The Hanley Chronicles

Also by G.H. Monroe

The Ramblings of a Lonely Stranger
A poetry collection

G.H. Monroe

The Hanley Chronicles

GHMonroe.com

Published by GHMonroe.com

All of the characters in this book are fictitious, and any resemblance to actual persons, living or dead, is purely coincidental.

ISBN 978-0-9980783-2-8
ISBN 978-0-9980783-3-5 (E-Book)
Copyright © 2021 by G.H. Monroe
All Rights Reserved
Printed in the United States of America
October 2021
First Edition

This book is dedicated to my parents, Wesley Monroe Jr. and Elizabeth Monroe, My daughter, and my granddaughter.

I would also like to thank the people who contributed to the creation of this novel, including but not limited to Aleathia Drehmer, Mike Duty, Kris Moulaison, Tyler Nichols, Lydia Orr, Mattea Orr, Vivian Orr, Michelle Pointis-Burns, Michelle Wells, and Peg Wood.

The Hanley Chronicles

CHAPTER ONE

Big Oak
(Told by Josh)

Being new in a small town is never easy, and looking back, the summer I turned eleven was no different. The fact that we didn't actually live in the village didn't help matters. It's hard to make friends in a new place when the only people you see are your parents.

The old Hanley place was a mile and a half outside the village. We'd moved there because my dad wanted to return to the rural life that he'd known in his youth. He wanted to become a farmer, as *his* father had been. Mom and I weren't crazy about the idea, but she promised me he'd grow out of it.

I didn't admit it to anyone, but I fell in love with the farm the very first time I laid eyes on it. With its sprawling fields, big red barn, old tractors, and the knee-high, stacked-stone wall that marked the perimeter of our property, it was everything I'd hoped a farm would be and ten times more. The wall was unbroken, except for the opening at the end of our long, straight driveway, and the two chained off gaps, on the west and south sides, used for getting tractors on and off the road. On the west side, not far from that opening, there was also a small gap where a foot trail onto our

6

property crossed the wall. It was an easy way for someone walking or riding a bike to get onto Nichols Corners Road from our property without messing with the chain.

The dirt driveway came onto the property off DeLeon Road. It crossed a bridge made of eight by eights, spanning the trickle of a stream that ran out from Grout Brook, which started in the woods west of our driveway. The driveway stretched the length of a football field, or perhaps one and a half, from the road to the two-story farmhouse. It ended in an oval loop around a large pine tree, no more than ten feet from the front porch. A lesser road branched off of that loop and led to the outbuildings, the largest of which was the big, red barn, standing fifty feet west of the house.

I would later come to learn that this barn held a terrible secret. However, when we first moved to the farm, the barn was nothing more to me than a magical place that was obviously made for a kid to have endless fun. The entire second floor was a fort that the grown-ups called a hayloft. I would re-position the smaller bales of hay, forming labyrinths, where I would play for hours on end.

The ladder that ascended to the loft was fun, but I soon discovered that the only *real* way to come down was the tight, two-inch-thick rope that stretched from loft to ground. It was attached to big hooks set in thick beams, one on the side wall up in the loft, and one on the ground floor wall, behind the bales of hay that sat by the door. My mother nearly blew a capillary the first time she saw me grab the big rolling pulley hook and zip-line down to the ground floor. Bent at the waist, I had my legs straight out in front of me as I zoomed down to the first floor, and stuck the landing, dead center of the hay bales.

At dinner, I threw out my chest as Mom told Dad all about what I had done.

Unimpressed with my swashbuckling flair, Dad just rolled his eyes and shook his head. "If you break your arm goofing off, don't think you're getting out of doing any chores," he said without batting an eye as he reached for the mashed potatoes.

The barn was all about fun, but chores were another matter altogether. As a kid who'd become accustomed to his chores consisting of cleaning his room and taking out the trash, I found the adjustment to farm life to be inconvenient at best. As far as chores went, I longed for those halcyon days of suburban paradise that I'd left behind. Here, it seemed like each time I found a way to manage my work so it ate up less of my fun time, Dad would pile on a handful more chores.

On the plus side, once we were moved in and more comfortable on the farm, Mom began to let me ride my bike into town to run errands for her. Soon, I got to know some of the local kids. I met Elijah Morley on one such trip to Clark's General Store.

Eli, as he preferred to be called, was a tall skinny kid with a bright red crew cut, elfin ears, and an impish grin that hinted at the mischief lurking just below the surface. His eyes always looked half shut, as if he was about to nod off, but trust me … Eli was always alert, and on the lookout for any potential tomfoolery.

It turned out that he lived on Nichols Corners Road, which runs perpendicular to DeLeon Road, the road we lived on. The Morley's place was one of the closest farms to ours, and so we became fast friends. In short order, we were inseparable. One frequently ate at, and slept over at the other one's house, and we burned most of our daylight hours fishing or exploring the small tract of woods that stood between our houses. Our moms often packed lunches, which we ate under the cool shade of the big oak tree by the pond that lay near the edge of our west field.

This was *our* spot, which came to be known as Big Oak.

From there, we could see both of our houses, and my mom quickly figured out that this was our preferred spot. She developed a system to communicate with me when I was out at Big Oak. She flew a yellow towel on the clothesline when I only had an hour more to play, and a big red beach towel as a signal for me to come on home right away.

Eli and I had many a deep philosophical discussion at Big Oak. Those discussions covered everything from the best bait for catching sunfish in the pond, to what happens after you die.

On a sunny afternoon in September, not long before school started, we were out at Big Oak. Eli sat with his back against a big rock, tossing acorns at an old black milk can that was half-buried in the ground as he told me the story about Mr. Hanley.

"You know about what happened on your farm, don't ya?" Eli asked between sips of root beer.

"No. What happened?"

"Mister Hanley, the man that lived here before you, got killed – shot dead, right there in the doorway of the barn!"

"Oh go on! You're jerking my chain, aren't you?" I said, not believing him for an instant.

"Swear on my mamma's grave!" There was no hint of the mischievous smile that usually indicated that someone's leg was being pulled. "Police chief found him there, face up in the dirt with a big hole in his chest. They say his eyes were wide open."

The grim look on Eli's face as he stared into the dirt convinced me that this was serious business.

"Why would someone shoot him? What happened?" I asked, afraid of what I might hear. Was my family in danger? Did my dad know about this when he bought the house?

"No one knows for sure. Word around town is that Mr. Lowery killed him over the treasure."

"Who's Mr. Lowery? What treasure?"

"Folks say there's treasure somewhere on this property, and Mr. Lowery was trying to steal it. Mr. Lowery was a friend of his. Well, at least he was until he shot him."

"Did anybody *see* him shoot Mr. Hanley?"

"Don't think so. But the newspapers said he did it."

"What kind of treasure? Gold? Money?" I asked, now dazed by the prospect of boundless wealth and fortune.

"Nobody knows. Some folks think it was money from a bank robbery that happened a while back. Some say it was just his life savings. I figure it had to be something pretty valuable for a man to get killed over it," Eli reasoned.

"So I got a treasure on my property," I muttered.

My mind tore through the possibilities. I was a man on a mission now. There was treasure to be found, and I was just the guy to find it. As I stared off into the distance, I noticed the red, 'get your butt home' towel flying from our clothesline. I had to go, but before we headed home, Eli and I agreed to meet at Big Oak the next morning.

Riding my bike home that evening, I saw everything

through new eyes. I looked at every tree as a possible marker, indicating where treasure might be hidden. I thought about the walls on the perimeter of the farm and how there were spots where the rocks were newer. Was one of those spots the place where poor, dead Mr. Hanley had stashed the loot?

CHAPTER TWO

The Dinner Table
(Told by Josh)

At dinner that night, the conversation started out in the usual, lighthearted manner. Mom passed along the gossip that the ladies in town had shared while Dad smiled politely and pretended to care. When it was his turn, Dad discussed the most recent farming trials, triumphs, and his plans for the future while Mom feigned interest. Meanwhile, I sat quietly, poking at my corn and waiting for the proper moment to drop my bomb.

"I want to re-paint that barn after I get all the fields turned," Dad said eagerly.

I never could figure out why Dad would get excited about a long list of work to be done. I'd always thought grownups were an odd bunch, and Dad wasn't doing anything to dispel that notion. Though she smiled and listened, Mom's lack of interest in the excruciating details of farming amused me and left me an opening to hit them with my earth-shattering revelation.

"Eli says Mr. Hanley got killed, right outside the barn," I blurted out.

The room fell dead silent and my parents looked at one another like two kids hoping the other one wasn't going to squeal.

Since both of them had apparently been struck mute, I kept on talking. "He says the Chief of Police found him by the barn door with a big hole in his chest."

Dad took his cue from the nervous look on Mom's face and spoke up.

"Does that bother you, Josh?" he asked with an unsettling calm.

"I guess it scares me a little bit. I don't want us to get killed too."

"Well Josh, the man who did the killing can't hurt us. While he was trying to get away from the Chief, he pointed his gun at him too, and the Chief had to shoot him. So he's gone, he can't hurt anyone else."

My jaw fell open. "You knew about all this Dad?"

"Yes, Josh. Your mother and I knew. That's why we got such a good price on this place. Mr. Hanley didn't have any family so the county was stuck with it. They sold it to us for a really good price because folks were afraid to live here. I guess they didn't know us very well. We aren't much afraid of anything, right son?"

"Right, Dad!" I said, not entirely convinced, but drawing a degree of courage from my father's words. "Why'd he kill Mr. Hanley?" I asked, poking at my meatloaf.

"No one really knows."

"Eli says he was after Mr. Hanley's treasure."

"I've heard stories like that too," Mom said, breaking her silence.

"I wonder where it's hidden," I added.

"Whoa there, Josh," Dad cautioned. "We don't even know if there *is* a treasure."

I nodded, but I was having *none* of it. I was convinced there was a treasure, and I was determined to find it.

The next day I met Eli at Big Oak and we rode our bikes into town. We went to the library to look up the details of Mr. Hanley's demise and maybe ask some adults what happened. Adults know everything.

CHAPTER THREE

Amy
(Told by Josh)

When Eli and I went into the little red brick library, we were dumbstruck. The librarian wasn't like any librarian I'd ever seen before. All of those librarians were at school, and they were cranky old hags who seemed to hate the whole world, but most especially, young boys. This librarian was different.

She had these huge brown eyes that I would have made fun of if she was any girl my own age, but on a grownup girl, they were just plain pretty. She kept her brown hair tied into a ponytail that ran halfway down her back. She wasn't dressed like a real librarian either. She wore a pair of blue jeans and a shirt with Bugs Bunny on it. Really, I'm not kidding! It was a Bugs Bunny shirt. She looked more like the girl who used to baby-sit me in our old town than a librarian. She greeted us with a warm smile and seemed genuinely happy to have us visit the library. I figured not many people came into the tiny library. Maybe she was just happy to have any company at all.

"Good morning, boys," she said, seemingly unaware that a library was supposed to be a quiet place.

"Good morning, ma'am," I whispered. I was used to getting

13

yelled at for talking in the school library, "We're looking for newspapers about how Mr. Hanley got killed."

Her smile evaporated.

"Oh my! Why would nice boys like you want to know about such an awful thing?"

"Well ma'am," Eli said, "Josh here moved into the old Hanley farm and I was telling him what happened to Mr. Hanley, and all about the treasure. So we came to the library to find out more."

"Oh, a couple of treasure hunters, huh?"

"Well, we want to know about the whole thing, but yes ma'am, we would like to know about the treasure too," I said, still whispering. I mean, who *doesn't* want to find a treasure?

"My name is Amy," she said as she stood up to shake hands with each of us, "not ma'am, and I appreciate you being nice and quiet, but when no one else is in the library, you don't have to whisper. As long as it's just us three, we can talk in our normal voices. You'll hear the bell on the door ding when somebody comes in. Now, would you boys like a soda?"

"Yes please," we answered in eager unison.

"Okay, have a seat and I'll be right back," she instructed, pointing to the table near her desk.

As we sat there, Eli and I scanned the room with the inquisitive eyes of youth. The room was filled with a heady aroma of books, the smell of knowledge. There were individual books sitting atop the card catalogs and on a few display tables as if to say, "We are special. You should read us."

I wondered who picked out the books that were displayed. Who decided which books were the special ones?

The paper flowers that hung on the wall with first names hand-printed on them were obviously made by little kids. That made me wonder when the little kids had been in the library. Did kids actually come here in the summer?

It began to dawn on me that a library was not much different from a school. But it was like a school that people came to because they wanted to. How twisted is that?

"I hope everyone likes root beer," Amy chirped when she returned to the table, somehow juggling three bottles of root beer and several newspapers.

She laid the newspapers down on the chair next to hers, twisted the tops off the root beers, gave one to me, one to Eli, took a sip of the third, and sat down with us. We got to know one another while drinking root beers before we got around to talking about Mr. Hanley. She had some questions; where I'd moved from, and how I liked it here. I told her how my dad said we'd gotten a good price on the Hanley farm because the county couldn't find any relatives or buyers. She seemed genuinely interested in what I had to say. It felt really good to have an adult talk to me and listen to me like what I had to say mattered. She didn't leave Eli out. She asked him how we met and what kind of adventures we were finding this summer.

The time passed so easily, we almost forgot why we'd come to the library in the first place. We even found ourselves quizzing *her*. I asked how she could be a librarian when she was so young. She laughed, told me she probably wasn't as young as I thought she was, and explained that she had recently graduated from college and she got the job here. She didn't have any family in town, and when she wasn't at work, she didn't do much besides read and play with her dog, Max.

We really liked Amy a lot, and it didn't hurt that she was pretty either. That friendly smile and those huge eyes made my stomach churn like it never had before.

"Now, about Mr. Hanley. Let's start by getting the facts, okay?" she said, unfolding one of the newspapers.

The headline, dated the eighth of April, 1984, declared in huge type, *Local Man Murdered*. Amy leaned back and reached over to her desk to get a yellow notepad and a pencil, both of which she handed to Eli.

"Will you keep notes, Eli?"

Without a word, he eagerly snatched the pad and pencil from her and poised himself to take down whatever would be deemed noteworthy. She handed the newspaper to me and asked me if I would read the story.

I was never too crazy about reading out loud. When I was younger, I had a pretty bad lisp. I eventually got over my lisp, but the kids at my old school had made fun of me so relentlessly, that I never liked to read out loud after that. But I couldn't say no to Amy.

I took the paper and started to read. She would occasionally stop me to point out the important facts of the stories and Eli would jot them down. We did that all afternoon, stopping only when the phone rang, the mailman came in, or our root beers ran dry and needed to be replaced.

She taught us about who, what, where, when, and why. We went through the stories in every newspaper and extracted the who, the what, the where, and the when from each story. Eli and I didn't say anything, but we shared a glance that held the same unspoken question. Where were the whys? None of the papers said anything about why Mr. Hanley had been killed at his barn by Rance Lowery. There was nothing about the why … the treasure! Amy caught us in that glance and knew exactly what we were thinking. She let us dangle for a short time before she chuckled and spoke up.

"But what about the treasure. That's what you guys are thinking … right?"

"Well," I answered, ashamed of my greed, "yeah, we *are* here to learn about the treasure."

"Okay guys, what we just got from the papers were the facts. No one knows the truth about the treasure, but I'll tell you what I've heard."

Just then the phone rang again. Based on Amy's half of the phone conversation, I knew who was calling.

"Yes ma'am, they are." There was a pause. "No, not at all, they have been perfect little gentlemen, and I am thoroughly enjoying their company," another pause. "Yep, I'll tell him," then the last pause. "Okay, buh-bye."

When she hung up, I didn't even give her time to say it. "My mom wants us home, right?"

"Yes, she said I should tell you that she made fried chicken and apple pie so maybe you'll get home on time today," Amy said with that pretty smile. "You boys come back tomorrow and I'll tell you what I've heard about the treasure, okay? But for now, you better hurry home so you can have your pie. I'm jealous, I love apple pie."

Eli and I tried to help clean the table, but Amy chased us away.

"You two don't worry about the table. I'll clean it up. If you get in trouble for being late, your moms might not let you come see me anymore!"

The bell above the door announced our exit as we waved goodbye to our new friend and hopped on our bikes to head home for dinner.

CHAPTER FOUR

A View From Above
(Told by Josh)

The next morning, time couldn't pass quickly enough. I was up with the roosters, and couldn't wait to get to the library. I'm not sure if it was the fact that we were finally going to talk about the treasure, or if I was just eager to see Amy again. At dinner the night before, Mom told me the library opened at ten in the morning. I knew it would be a long wait from sunrise until ten o'clock, so when I woke up, I got busy doing chores in hopes that it would make the time pass more quickly. I took out the trash, cleaned out chicken coops, turned over the soil and pulled weeds in Mom's garden and flowerbeds, all the while running inside every twenty minutes to check the time. When I ran out of chores, I took a bath and asked Mom what else I could do. She asked me to clean some things out of the barn. There were still some of Mr. Hanley's things out there, and since no one had come for them, she wanted me to take them down to the basement, which I set to doing without complaint. When I got down to the basement with the first load of stuff, Mom was down there.

"Who are you, and what have you done with my son?" she jokingly asked.

"What are we gonna do with his stuff?" I asked, ignoring her sarcasm.

"We should keep it for a little while. I know Mr. Hanley has no family, but I just think it's disrespectful to be in a big hurry to throw out a person's belongings after they die."

I gazed longingly at his fishing tackle. It sat in the corner by six blue, plastic, five-gallon jugs of water. "I guess you're right Mom."

"I think you're going to have to fight your father for that fishing gear anyway. He has his eye on that too."

Not long after I'd started moving Mr. Hanley's things, I heard muffled voices upstairs while I was in the basement. As they got nearer to the top of the basement stairs, Eli's voice became recognizable. "Thanks, Mrs. Corey." I heard the door to the basement open. "Hey Josh, are you down there? Are you ready to head into town?"

"Yep! I been ready since sunrise. I got one last bunch of stuff in the barn to bring down here. I'll be right up."

While we ran out to the barn, Mom got a Tupperware container out of the fridge and put it inside of a brown paper bag. Once we had the last load of stuff, mostly boxes with books and pictures, put away in the cellar, we tore back up the stairs and towards the back door. With one, 'Are you running in the house?' look, Mom, stopped us in our tracks.

I gave her a sheepish smile. "Uhm … sorry, Mom."

"Here," she said, allowing a slight smile to cross her lips as she handed me the brown paper bag.

"What's this?" I asked, peeking inside.

"It's a piece of apple pie for your librarian friend, Amy. Anyone who can get you two to sit still in a library all day and come back the next day for more, deserves a piece of apple pie."

As hard as I tried, I couldn't suppress my grin. I'm pretty sure Mom knew then and there, that I was sweet on Amy, even though I might not have realized it yet myself.

* * *

As we entered the library, the jingle of the bell made Amy look at the door. When she saw us, she put down her book and smiled a 'glad to see you' smile.

"Hey boys. I wondered if I'd scared you away forever."

"I brought you some pie," I proudly told her as I handed her the bag. "Mom said anyone who could keep us still in a library all day deserved a piece of pie."

"Aw, you tell your mom I said thank you so much. Are you boys drinking root beer today?"

"We sure are!" came the answer in the same eager, eleven-year-old stereo, as we both took our seats at our designated work table. Amy sat her pie down and went out back to get a round of sodas, our notes from yesterday, and a fork.

"So, where were we?" she asked as she opened the Tupperware.

"You were going to tell us what you heard about the treasure," Eli answered before I could.

"Ah yes," she recalled, "now you have to understand that what we got out of the paper were facts," she cautioned, waving the note pad from the previous day to make her point. "What I'm about to tell you today is mostly rumors and speculation. You understand the difference, right?"

"Yes, yes, we get it," I said. I was impatient. I was ready for her to get to the good stuff.

She handed the notepad and pen to Eli and took a bite of pie.

"Okay, here's the deal. I go to the Main Street Diner most every morning for coffee before I come to work. A few days after Mr. Hanley was killed, I was having my coffee when a couple of village police officers and another man sat in the booth behind me." She took another bite of pie. "I didn't see the third man, but I recognized his voice. He was Mr. Cosgrove, the man who runs the antique shop.

I had my head down because I had a headache, so I guess they thought I was asleep, or I wasn't paying attention, but I heard them talking. One of the policemen had been out to the Hanley farm, and he was telling the others what he saw. He said that Mr. Lowery, the man who killed Mr. Hanley, must have gone all through the house and the barn looking for something. He said it was obvious that whatever it was Lowery wanted, he wanted it really bad. Then he said he was gonna check the rest of the farm out before anybody new moved in. I guess I've been a little curious about the whole thing since then." Amy smiled and took another bite of pie.

"Check the rest of the farm for what?" I asked, hoping it was something other than my treasure.

Eli turned to me. "The treasure, you goober, what do ya think? That must have been why I kept seeing the police car out at your place before you guys moved in. He spent a lot of time looking in the house and the barn. I thought he was just investigating the killin'."

"Maybe he already found the treasure," I said, my voice betraying a bit of concern, "maybe it's gone."

"When was the last time you saw the police car?" Amy asked Eli.

"The day before Josh moved in."

"Well then, I'd say if he was still hunting up until then, I don't think he found whatever he was looking for," Amy said. "What I would do, is make a map of the property and mark off each place that you check. Look in and around the buildings first. Have you found any old things of Mr. Hanley's?"

"Yeah, my mom had me move a bunch of his stuff down to the cellar this morning. There was no treasure, mostly boxes of books, papers, and pictures."

"I would go through all of that," Amy said. "What if he made a map, or notes about something he hid somewhere? Also, the more you know about Mr. Hanley, the better your chances are, of finding something he might have hidden."

Just then, the bell jingled and two people came in. Amy went back to the front desk, and Eli and I set to the task of drawing a map, and making notes of all the places on the property we thought were worth checking. We immediately discovered that we weren't very good at map-making, so we decided to write down the list of places that we already checked first. We'd get back to drawing the map later. We burned the next several hours at these tasks while Amy ate her pie and did some of her regular library work. She must have seen our futile attempts at map-making, and decided to help us. On her way back from where the printers and copiers were, she stopped and dropped several sheets of paper on our table. They were pictures of our farm. They looked like they'd been taken from a plane flying over, just like danged spy pictures! Not only was Amy pretty, she was probably a darn secret agent too. How cool was that?

"How did you *do* that?" I asked breathlessly.

"I copied them from the Environmental Conservation field guide," she said, "they take aerial photos for the USDA every year. They make copies for us too. The farmers use them to plan their crops."

"This is *so* cool!" I stammered as Eli took the pictures from me to get a closer look. Amy was pointing to some of the interesting features and explaining them when Eli interrupted her to point out something that helped to date the photo.

"Look, in the driveway. There's the truck that Mr. Hanley bought last year. I used to see it when I came into town."

"And our new shed behind the house isn't in the picture there," I added.

"There's the path to the back forty," Eli pointed to the path that Dad used to get the tractor out to this side of the back fields.

"Yes, you can see how the paths are worn into the ground," Amy added. "Look on the other side of the property, there's another path that leads from the house out to that little pond on the edge of the trees. What's out there?"

"Nothing much," I told her "that's where the woods come up to the big slate rock hill. He probably went hunting or fishing out there. It's a pretty place. We call it Big Oak."

Whatever it was, we had our notes from the newspaper and these incredible pictures, and all the way home we made plans for a full search of the property. It was going to be an exciting adventure.

CHAPTER FIVE

Girls … Ugh!
(Told by Josh)

All these years later, at Big Oak, the sunrise is still a work of art, painted in a thousand shades of yellow, blaze orange and gold, all on a blue canvas that spreads over our eastern field. I experienced the *full* majesty of this masterpiece for the first time on the morning after Amy gave us those incredibly cool aerial photos. As near as I recall, this was the first time in my young life that I had consciously, appreciated the serenity and splendor of a sunrise. I'd been up at that hour before, but I guess I just never paid attention to how beautiful it all was … until that day. Maybe that was simply the first time I was up that early and not doing some chore. As I stood at Big Oak inhaling the crisp autumn air, I watched an immense buck saunter up and take a drink from the pond.

My first moments spent in full awareness of the beauty of nature didn't last long. The buck jerked his head up from the pond and glared in my general direction. But I wasn't the one who disturbed the brawny deer. He'd been jarred from his drink by the rickety squeals and groans of a bicycle, coming up the trail behind me. This was the trail between Eli's house and Big Oak. In a blink, the big deer bolted off across the east field and into the thick woods at the far end.

"Hey, Josh. Eli said you'd be waiting for him here."

I whirled around to see who belonged to this unfamiliar voice. Who was the interloper trespassing on our spot and on my peaceful moment with nature? I could scarce believe my eyes when I saw a *girl*. She wasn't much taller than me, and she was skinny with short dark hair and big eyes, like a frog. I'd seen her around town before but I didn't know her name and didn't really care to. She wasn't like Amy; she was just a skinny girly girl. What in blazes was she doing at Big Oak? She might as well have been in the men's room at the Pentagon! This was *our* spot, mine and Eli's. Who had given her clearance to be here?

"I don't care what that dope says. That treasure is on my property and I decide who gets to hunt it with me. And another thing, this is our secret spot and you got no business coming here. No girls are allowed! Ya hear?"

"Treasure? You guys are hunting for treasure?" she asked with heightened interest.

"I was just riding my bike to town," she said. "Eli told me this was a good shortcut. He said you'd be here and asked me to tell you his dad gave him a few extra chores and he'd be a little late. He never said anything about any treasure."

It occurred to me then, that I might be quicker with my mouth than with my brain.

I rolled my eyes. *Ugh, me and my big mouth!*

"You blabbermouth," came Eli's voice from behind me. "She didn't know a thing about the treasure. Josh Corey, meet Mary Fran Barker. She's my neighbor on the other side. Mary Fran, this is my frog-mouthed friend, Josh."

"Hey, Josh," she said for the second time in the last several minutes.

Her voice was still cordial, a lot more cordial than I deserved after my outburst. I muttered some grumpy, insincere greeting and started hashing through all of the possible ways that we might be able to keep this … this … girl out of our inner circle. Short of homicide, there seemed to be no easy way to do so at this point. Girls are famous for being blabbermouths, I reasoned, thus justifying my desire to exclude her. I didn't fully appreciate the irony of that line of thought.

"You can help us hunt up the treasure if you want, but you have to keep your mouth shut. We don't want people swarming all over my property trying to steal our treasure."

"So, what you're telling me … is not to be a frog-mouth?" Mary Fran said with a smart-alecky grin while Eli tried to conceal his giggle.

I didn't like girls very much.

"Do you want in, or don't you?" I demanded, watching Eli's stupid smirk out of the corner of my eye.

"Yeah, that sounds like fun. We split everything three ways right?"

"Yeah, yeah, fine ... three ways." I conceded grudgingly.

"Okay, well I still have to go to town for my mom. Then I have to do a couple of chores, I should be back in about an hour," she said.

"We'll be at my house," I pointed up the trail towards home. "Knock on the door and tell my mom I told you it was alright for you to come over."

"Okay, I'll see you guys then," she said before riding up the trail toward my house and town.

"What the heck did you let her in on it for?" Eli asked after Mary Fran was out of earshot.

"Well, I had to, after she knew about the treasure."

"Everybody knows the rumor about the treasure, you bonehead."

"Why'd you send her up the trail to our spot? Everyone doesn't know about our spot. If you hadn't sent her up here, it never woulda happened."

Eli didn't have an answer for *that,* which left me a small measure of vindication. With order restored, we planned our hunt for riches as we walked through the morning mist. The birds chirped and flew about as the warming rays of the early September sun burned off the fog.

CHAPTER SIX

Grout Brook
(Told by Josh)

In the basement, Eli and I got busy following Amy's suggestions to study Mr. Hanley's belongings. Eli took the pen and notebook, and we began going through the boxes of things that once belonged to Mr. Hanley. The first box was filled mostly with old pictures. Some were black and white, and others had the rusty hues that characterize older photos. A few of the photos, the most recent, were in color. The people in the photographs were surely related. Based on the newspaper photos I'd seen of Mr. Hanley in the library, there was an eerily strong resemblance between the men in the older pictures and the recently departed Mr. Hanley. Clearly, some of the photos had to be of Mr. Hanley's father and his grandfather.

The photos were mostly taken on and around the farm. We both recognized many of the locations. There were several photos taken of Hanley men, fishing at Grout Brook, a short, but surprisingly substantial stream that ran for about two-hundred-fifty yards through the woods in the northwest corner of our property. I immediately recognized the fly rod and reel in one of the photos as the same stuff that I had first seen in the basement the previous day. That very same fly-fishing equipment leaned against the wall not more than five feet from where Eli and I sat. I was glad we still had it. Something seemed right about it still being here on this farm.

There was what I figured was a picture of Mr. Hanley's father, posing with a beautiful blonde woman on the porch. I wondered if she was still alive. The only difference I could see in the house between then and now, was that the picture was black and white, and the porch swing wasn't there in the picture. So I told Eli to write down that the Hanley's had lived here for a long time.

"How long?"

"How the heck am I supposed to know?" I grumbled.

Just then, we heard the front door open upstairs. We both cringed at the sound of my mother welcoming a visitor with a girl's voice and directing her to the basement stairs. It could only be one person.

"Hey, guys," came the voice from the top of the basement stairs.

"Hi, Mary Fran," we answered in unison with all of the enthusiasm one might muster for a vaccination.

"So what are we doing?" she asked, oblivious to our lack of excitement about her arrival.

"We're going through Mr. Hanley's things," I told her, "Amy said we should go through his things to learn as much as we could about him."

"Who's Amy?"

"She's the librarian in town. Jeez, don't you ever read?" Eli sounded so indignant, you might have thought that he was an avid reader of anything more profound than the backs of baseball cards.

Though I was completely in favor of any sarcasm directed toward this bothersome girl, I was amused by the fact that perhaps the only person in the world less literate than I, was chastising her for not being well-read.

"Does this belong to Mr. Hanley?" she asked, taking the photograph from my hand.

"Yep. We figure it's probably a picture of his dad," Eli told her.

"Looks like it was taken right out in front of this house," she said, examining the photo, front and back.

Eli and I looked at each other and rolled our eyes. Girls! Masters of the obvious. I couldn't figure out why everybody thought they were so smart.

"You said the librarian told you to find out everything you could. What have you found out?"

"Well," Eli said, "his family lived here for a long time. Most all of these pictures were taken here on Josh's farm."

"What else?"

"That's it, that's all we found out," Eli said, showing her the notebook.

Girls! They could be so dumb sometimes!

"Well this picture was taken in 1935," she said like a know it all.

"How do *you* know?" I demanded, insisting that she back up her cocksure tone of voice with some sort of proof that she had *any* idea what she was talking about.

"Well first, look at the car! That's a 1935 Buick Model 4419. My daddy likes old cars. He has models and pictures of them and he's always showing them to me. He has a model of one of these on his desk. Second, look at the headline on the newspaper the man is holding. It says 'Will Rogers Killed in Plane Crash'. My mom watches old movies. She loved his movies; we watch them together a lot. Mom told me that Will Rogers died in 1935."

If Mary Fran hadn't been so busy studying that old picture, she might have noticed the slack-jawed amazement with which Eli and I gawked at her. Darn girls!

Thankfully, that was about the time Mom called us from upstairs. She said there was a dog roaming around the barn and she wanted Eli and Mary Fran to have a look out the window to see if they knew who it belonged to. We put down the things we were looking through and went upstairs, but by the time we got there the dog had run off.

We went back downstairs and back to the business of learning about Mr. Caleb Hanley, whose family had occupied this farm for at least seven decades, and who had fished the same hole on Grout Brook that my dad fished most every weekend.

As much as Eli and I hated to admit it, Mary Fran had been helpful. She was pretty smart … and she was beginning to grow on us.

CHAPTER SEVEN

That Stupid Grin
(Told by Josh)

Over the next several days, the three of us carefully went over the items in the basement. The task of learning about these things took us to the library more than once. On the first of these library visits, Mary Fran met Amy.

Amy waved. "Hey, guys."

"Hey, Amy, how are you?" Eli and I said.

"I am just dandy! I thought maybe you guys got tired of me. May I ask who this lovely young lady is?"

I *swear*, when Eli and I turned around and looked past Mary Fran to see what lovely, young lady Amy was talking about, we weren't trying to be funny, or smart-alecks, or anything like that. But just try and tell Mary Fran that. The look she gave us was like the look Mom gave me the time I brought the milk snake in the kitchen.

"Oh," I said in an honest moment of dawning, "you mean Mary Fran. She's Eli's neighbor. She lives on the other side of his place from me. I guess she's kinda helpin' us look for the treasure."

"I see," Amy smiled and extended a hand to Mary Fran,

"well I'm pleased to meet you, Mary Fran. My name is Amy. Can I offer you and your two smart-aleck friends some root beer?"

"Pleased to meet you too, ma'am," Mary Fran answered, shaking hands with Amy.

"My name is Amy, not ma'am. Now, how about those root beers?"

"Yes ma'a … I mean, yes please." Mary Fran said with a big grin.

As she came out of the back room with a round of root beers, Amy noticed the brown grocery bag that I was carrying.

"What have you got in there?" she asked.

In that bag, I carried the only piece of clothing that we'd found amongst the belongings of the late Mr. Hanley. It was a waist-length, olive green Army jacket with the name 'Hanley' on the chest and a patch sewn onto the left shoulder. The patch was black, with an angry looking eagle beneath an arched banner bearing the word 'airborne'.

"We thought we might be able to find out about this jacket if we brought it to the library. We figured you'd know something about it."

"Well Josh," she said, pulling the jacket from the bag to examine it. "It's definitely an army jacket. I think I know what this patch is, but let's look it up just to be sure."

Amy was so smart. She knew where to look up everything. She found a book that showed pictures of a bunch of patches that looked a lot like the one on our jacket. It took a little time, but she found a patch that was exactly like ours.

"This is a World War II jacket. The patch is the symbol of the 101st Airborne Division, also known as The Screaming Eagles. Those were the guys in the army who parachuted out of planes. It probably belonged to Mr. Hanley's father. I don't think Mr. Hanley was old enough to have been in World War II," she explained. "If Mr. Hanley was 45 when he died, that would have made him between two and six years old during World War II.

"Well that's two clues that ended up being nothing," Eli said.

"Huh? Two? What other clue are you talking about?" she asked, turning his way.

"Remember that path that was worn out to the creek? That's Grout Brook. We found a bunch of old pictures of Mr. Hanley fishing there. We figure there's no great treasure out there, just trout. We found pictures of him and his folks. They've lived there at least since 1935, and they were just going out there to fish, just like Josh and his dad."

Amy sounded surprised. "How'd you come up with 1935?"

That just made Mary Fran grin that stupid grin of hers. I hated that grin!

"Mary Fran figured it out by looking at some of the other old pictures," I grudgingly admitted.

"Wow. That's pretty impressive," she said, fawning all over Mary Fran. "How did you figure that out by looking at the pictures?"

"It wasn't no big thing," Mary Fran said bashfully. "There was a newspaper in the picture. I knew the date by the headline, and I recognized an old car that was in the picture too, well it wasn't old then, but it is now. My daddy likes old cars."

"What headline from 1935 did you recognize?"

"It was about Will Rogers dying. My mamma likes his movies. She knows everything about him."

"Oh!" Amy said with that trademark smile. "Aren't you a well-rounded girl! Well, I better quit yakking. I'm taking up your valuable treasure hunting time. You guys don't have much summer left to find that treasure. School starts on Monday."

Gasp! School? Was it time for school already? Where had the summer gone? Eli and I just stared at each other in horror for several seconds before we both, at the same instant, shifted our gaze towards Mary Fran. Ugh! There was that stupid grin again.

CHAPTER EIGHT

Ambushed
(Told by Josh)

Those last few days of summer passed like trash cans in a tornado, and before we knew it, it was Sunday, the last day of Summer. Boy, was the beginning of school going to put a serious crimp in our search for riches. Dad was going fishing down at Grout Brook, so we decided to ride down in the back of his truck and walk over to Big Oak from there. One last Big Oak meeting before school. As usual, we ended up talking about where we should look for the treasure.

"Well, we went through all the buildings. We know it's not in your house, the barn, any of the sheds, or in the old pump house." Mary Fran said from the thick branch where she hung upside down from bent legs.

"So now all we have to do is search the rest of the 210 acres of Josh's farm," Eli said with a blade of grass sticking from his mouth.

"How do you know how big our farm is?"

"My dad told me that the farms on this road are all the same size, 210 acres."

"You know," Mary Fran said, "we can eliminate most of

33

the property on the farm."

"And just how can we do that, Miss know-it-all?"

"Easy, Josh. Most of a farm is fields, and fields get turned every year with big old plows. Mr. Hanley wouldn't bury treasure someplace where the dirt gets turned over every year."

Once again, Eli and I found ourselves staring at each other like a couple of cavemen who had just seen fire for the first time. Neither of us wanted to admit it, but we were both thinking it. We were dumb as stumps and she was smart, and to be honest, she really wasn't that bad for a girl. My mother had told me all along that I could always bring my friends home for dinner, but I'd never invited Mary Fran. I'd always waited until she headed home to invite Eli. But that day, for some reason, I didn't wait.

I knew Dad had quit fishing because I'd heard his truck going back up the trail thirty minutes earlier. We were going to have to walk, and now my stomach was snarling.

"You guys wanna come over for dinner? My mom's cooking fried chicken, corn on the cob and mashed potatoes."

"Heck yeah," Eli answered almost immediately, "is she making apple pie?"

"She might be, I saw her peeling apples this morning. Mary Fran, you wanna come or not?"

"I didn't think you meant me too," she said in a soft, ragged voice, fighting back the gleam of a tear.

I had never before been snowed under by such an avalanche of guilt.

"Of course I meant you too, Mary Fran," I said, mustering as much sincerity as I could, "you're one of us. If we're all gonna be rich together we gotta be good friends, and good friends come over for dinner."

The smile that spread across her face told me I'd done a good thing.

"I gotta run home and ask my mom."

"My house is closer than your house. If you want, you can just walk over with Eli and me, and call her from there."

"Okay, Josh," she wiped away a tear, "thanks."

About then I noticed Eli's sideways glare of disapproval. But I didn't care what he thought. He didn't have to fight off that nausea of guilt that overcame me at the sight of those tears boiling up in her eyes. I felt the daggers of his stare all the way to my house, but when we hit the back door, the smell of Mom's fried chicken and apple pie melted that frost. Mary Fran had a little trouble getting the okay from her mom to stay for dinner. Apparently, her mom was worried about her walking home alone too close to dark. I thought this was silly. I mean, what could possibly happen to a kid between our house and Mary Fran's?

"Don't worry, Mrs. Barker," I shouted loud enough to be heard on the other end of the phone, "I'll walk her home."

That, apparently, was enough to turn the trick.

"Okay Mamma, thanks … yes, ma'am, we'll be careful … I love you too, Mamma," she said before hanging up.

Dinner was really fun, I had two friends now, and it was just in time. School would start the next day, and it would be much more survivable now that I could start it with a couple of friends. After dinner, we all sat on the front porch swing eating apple pie, watching the squirrels chase each other, and cracking jokes until Eli's mom swung by on her way home from town to pick him up. Mom came out and talked with her for a few minutes and then it was just Mary Fran and I.

A half-hour later, Mom offered to take Mary Fran home. Mary Fran started to answer, but I cut her off.

"No thanks, Mom. We don't mind the walk, and besides, I can use the exercise."

The sun slipped beneath the western horizon just as we walked past Big Oak, and for the second time in my life, I consciously recognized the beauty of the meeting of sun and horizon. This time I was aware of even more; the chirping of the crickets, the singing of the birds, and the smell of the wildflowers in the meadow. I silently wondered if all of this had always been here. How had I never noticed it before? Meanwhile, Mary Fran was talking about the treasure and what our next move should be. I wondered for a moment if the treasure was actually right in front of us. Could the treasure actually be this beautiful countryside all around us?

"… right, Josh? … Josh? Josh, are you listening?"

"Huh? Yeah, I'm listening … what'd you say?"

"I was saying that we should start checking the grounds around your house next," Mary Fran repeated. "If I had a treasure, I'd want to keep it where I could see it."

"Makes sense to me," I said, still not entirely engaged in the conversation.

The occasional kiss of a rising sunfish sent concentric ripples across the surface of the pond and the reflected image of the brilliant sunset. Nature's gallery had my attention, despite the best efforts of my chatty friend.

"So we're all meeting at Eli's house to catch the bus at seven-thirty tomorrow morning, right?" she asked.

"Yep." I said, still gazing at the surface of the pond.

Several minutes later, we cut across to the road and walked the last stretch along Nichols Corners Rd. to the end of her driveway.

"Thanks for letting me come to dinner tonight," she said.

"No problem, Mary Fran. I'm sorry if I made you feel bad before by not inviting you. I just figured you wouldn't wanna hang around with a couple of dumb old boys. I know how you girls hate us boys."

I was quite proud of how well I thought on my feet. That was a perfectly plausible explanation for having left her out before.

"I don't hate boys. Eli's nice, maybe a little goofy, but he's nice. And you're ..."

"I'm what?"

"Never mind." Then there was a stretch of silence louder and more uncomfortable than any I'd ever had in all my life.

"Mary Fran ... Come on in, honey. It's getting dark." Mrs. Barker hollered from the front door.

"Okay Mamma, I'll be right in."

The front door wasn't closed a fraction of a second when Mary Fran leaned forward and did it. Bang. Quick as a rattlesnake, she planted a kiss on my left cheek, turned around, and ran up her driveway.

"See you tomorrow morning at Eli's," she yelled over her shoulder without turning around.

I stood dumbstruck, at the end of the Barker's driveway

holding my left cheek thinking I *should* want to slug her, while at the same time, wishing she'd kissed me longer. I ran home, and sat on the front porch swing, by myself, with a queasy feeling in my stomach, watching fireflies and thinking about that kiss until Mom finally made me come in and get ready for bed.

CHAPTER NINE

The First Day
(Told by Josh)

The cool air of the autumn morning created condensation that rose from Eli's mouth as he spoke.

"Hey, Josh. You're early."

"Can you believe I couldn't wait?" I said, as we walked down his porch stairs and up his driveway.

"Weird, huh. We hate school so much but when it starts, we can't wait to get there," Eli said, half talking to me, and half talking to himself. "But I'm glad you came early. I got something I wanna tell you."

"Oh yeah? What's that?"

"I like Mary Fran," he said.

Awkward!

The words splashed into the pit of my stomach and sent waves of shudder through my whole body. How could he like her when *I* liked her? I mean she kissed *me*, not him. Or did she kiss him too? I couldn't tell Eli that I liked her too, or that she kissed me. Here he was, my best friend, and he just told me that he was sweet on a girl who'd kissed me the night before. This was a most uncomfortable set of events! What the heck was I supposed to say?

"Hey, guys," Mary Fran's voice simultaneously relieved my discomfort and added to it.

She popped out from the path that runs through the small stand of trees between her house and Eli's. Her mom preferred that she not walk on the road in the morning fog.

"Hey, Mary Fran." Eli beat me to the punch.

I just smiled at Mary Fran and we all continued up the driveway to the road with Mary Fran walking between Eli and me.

"My mom said you should tell your mother thanks again for havin' me over for dinner," she said, sneaking a smile my way.

"Josh's mom is really a good cook, isn't she?" Eli chimed in.

"I'll tell her," I said, hanging my head to hide my face from her affectionate gaze.

I could feel the warm blush climbing my face under her predatory gaze and impish smile. I didn't want to look goofy, and I certainly didn't want Eli to see me looking all moon-eyed at the girl he'd just confessed to liking. Geez, no wonder I didn't like girls. They complicate *everything*. My stomach got all knotted up when Mary Fran veered right to avoid a puddle in the driveway and bumped against me. I really needed someone or something to break the tension I was feeling at that moment. Thank God the bus pulled up and we had to run to the end of the driveway, saving me from a situation that was getting more awkward by the moment.

I avoided Eli and Mary Fran all day at school, going so far as to miss the bus on purpose so I didn't have to deal with any thorny seating situations. Mom picked me up at school and ran a few errands on the way home. Meanwhile, as I waited in the car, I did the reading I'd been assigned in class that day, and my stomach churned at the thought of Eli sitting next to Mary Fran on the bus. I was torn, incredibly glad I hadn't taken the bus ... and wishing like heck I was on that darn bus.

"Are you okay sweetie?" Mom asked as we walked up the porch steps.

"Yeah Mom, I'm okay."

"You seem a little out of sorts. Is everything okay between you and Eli?"

God! How did she know? Sometimes I thought my mom had some

sort of super, mother, mind-reading powers or something.

"Sure Mom, everything's great. Where's Dad?"

"I think he's out at the brook, up where it starts. I saw him messing around with his fly-fishing gear this morning. He's been scuffling to get ahead of his work all weekend, I think he's been planning to do some fishing."

I went out to the garage and grabbed my spinning rod and a small box of spoons and spinners. Then I hopped on my bike and rode down the trail to Grout Brook where I found Dad's truck parked fifty feet from the water.

Grout Brook was a peculiar stream. It ran over a hundred and twenty feet wide in places, and was too deep to see the bottom in many spots. What made it odd, was that a stream of that width and depth wasn't much more than a couple of football fields long, and then it just disappeared into the ground. The fishing in Grout Brook would have been considered a treasure to a lot of people. Dad always said that this little creek had some of the best trout fishing he'd ever seen.

I put my bike in the bed of Dad's pickup and walked down the trail to the Brook. I worked my way up to where Dad was fishing in the deep pool upstream. His small streamer, made of duck feathers, rode downstream through the crystal clear water, over the slate rocks, and into the aqua-colored depths. Dad squinted to follow the path of his line as it floated downstream.

"Hey son, how was school?" he asked, not bothering to turn around.

"It was okay," I said, arching a long cast diagonally upstream.

I bounced the silver spoon along the bottom as it swung downstream. With a grunt, Dad set the hook into what was obviously a very large fish. I reeled in my lure as fast as I could and grabbed the net from the rock where Dad had set it down. I waited while he did battle with the unseen monster of a fish.

"Something on your mind?" Dad asked as he held the throbbing rod tip high.

"Mary Fran kissed me last night," I blurted out with no lead-in or fanfare.

"Well, I guess that can be a good thing or a bad thing. How

do you feel about it?"

"I guess I liked it okay," I said after pondering the question for a few moments, "but then this morning Eli told me that he likes her."

"Oh," my dad said as the enormous fish thrashed to the surface thirty feet away, "does Eli know that Mary Fran kissed you?"

"No way! I was gonna tell him at the bus stop this morning, but the dope told me that he liked her before I got the chance. I think it would really hurt his feelings if he knew she kissed me; especially now, after he told me he likes her."

Dad pondered my dilemma as his reel screeched and the fish bulldogged his way back into the depths.

"Seems to me that you have two choices, either you tell Mary Fran that you don't like her that way, or you tell Eli what happened. I imagine he'll eventually figure it out on his own anyway, and he'll probably be even more hurt if he finds out on his own."

"I guess you're right Dad," I sighed.

Dad's fish was twenty-four inches long and it wasn't even the biggest one we caught that evening. This little brook in the middle of our farm seemed to be teeming with huge trout. We caught, photographed, and released more than a dozen trout over twenty-two inches before driving back home under another magnificent September sunset.

At home, I sat on the front porch swing watching the sun finish its show, and thinking about how to break the news to Eli.

CHAPTER TEN

Stray
(Told by Josh)

My stomach tightened the next morning as I left home and walked towards Eli's house.

What will I say? What if he gets mad and takes a poke at me?

As I walked past Big Oak, my preoccupation with this troubling issue prevented me from taking notice of the stray dog that had begun to follow me. It had to be that same stray Mom saw a few days ago. I didn't notice its silent approach until it was only a few feet away from me. Fortunately for me, it was a friendly dog, because if it had a mind to, the dog could have gotten a sizable chunk of my leg before I saw it. After nearly jumping out of my shoes, I introduced myself to the wandering canine that I quickly determined was female.

"Hey, girl," I knelt down to greet her. "don't you have a home?"

She was almost all black, with a shock of white fur on her chest. Her pointy, alert ears and proud, assertive walk made her look like anything but a stray. She might have been lost or homeless, but she wasn't without self-assurance. I had the distinct

42

feeling that I was the stray and she was finding me. With no second thoughts, I opened my lunch, dug out my peanut butter and jelly sandwich, and offered it to her. Without hesitation, she accepted my offering and scarfed it down in three big gulps. That sealed it, I had a friend for life. She pranced alongside as I ran back towards home. Mom was none too pleased to see me heading back towards home and away from the bus stop, *and* with this stray dog in tow.

"Are you lost, young man? The school bus is that way," she said, pointing towards Eli's house.

"She was gonna follow me to the bus, Mom. I didn't want to leave her sittin' down by the road where a car could hit her."

"Well ... okay ... she can stay in the barn until you get home, but then you'll have to find out where her home is and get her there. If you can't find out where she lives, we'll have to take her to the pound. Understand?"

"Yes ma'am," I said with my head hung.

Just then we heard the rumble of the school bus in the distance. Mom rolled her eyes.

"Put the dog in the barn and get in the car."

"Uhm Mom ..."

"Yes?"

"I uhm ... gave her my sandwich."

Between Dad and me, Mom rolled her eyes enough that I was sure she'd seen the inside of her own head several times. Though she rolled her eyes and gasped in exasperation, I knew she wasn't mad at me. I had learned quite a while before then, that when she sighed and rolled her eyes that way, Mom was more annoyed at herself for being a soft touch than she was at me or Dad.

"Well, put her in the barn and get her some water while I make you another sandwich."

"Okay, Mom."

I brought an old blanket out to the barn and laid it atop a bed of hay in one of the old stalls where horses had once been kept. I sat a bucket of fresh water in the corner of the stall and gave her directions like I thought she understood me.

"Now you stay here girl. We'll find out where you live

43

when I get back from school."

All day at school I thought about my new friend. I worried that she might be gone by the time I got home, I went through possible names for her in my mind, completely ignoring that whole 'Find her home or she goes to the pound' discussion. I was so distracted that I almost forgot about the entire Eli and Mary Fran fiasco. That is until I got on the bus.

"Hey, Josh," Mary Fran hollered from the back of the bus where she sat in the window seat next to some other girl who I didn't know, but who I was eternally grateful to.

"Hey, Mary Fran … hey, Eli," I said, plopping down in the seat Eli had saved for me next to his own.

"Where were you this morning? You missed the bus."

That stray dog my mom saw started following me halfway to the bus stop. I didn't want her to follow me down there and get left by the road."

"So what did ya do with her?"

"I took her back to my house and put her in my barn."

"That is so cool, you have a dog."

"Not so fast," I said, "my mom told me I had to find out where the dog lived and take her home or else she had to go to the pound."

"Can we help?" Mary Fran asked.

For a moment I'd forgotten that she was there.

"Sure," I said, forgetting for that instant how the three of us running around together might get prickly.

But what was done was done. It was gonna be Eli, Mary Fran and me, same as always.

CHAPTER ELEVEN

Her Name is Penny
(Told by Josh)

When I got home, I ran out to the barn to see if the stray was still there. She was. Mom immediately came out and reminded me that my mission was to find the dog's home and get her back to it.

"I know, I know, Mom. I'm just waiting for Eli and Mary Fran to come over. They're gonna help me. They had to drop off their books and Mary Fran had to change outta her dress."

"Okay, I just wanted to be sure you didn't forget our agreement. After all, a deal's a deal."

"Nope, I didn't forget Mom. We'll get her home."

"Why don't you go in and change out of your school clothes. While you do that, I'll make a snack for you and your friends."

"Okay, Mom."

I didn't realize it, but when I ran in the house and up the stairs that clever dog was right behind me. I was a bit startled to find her there when I turned to close my bedroom door. To this day, I'm not exactly sure how she got past Mom and into the house. But there she was at my bedroom door. She strolled in, sat quietly in the corner of my room with her head cocked to one side, and watched me get changed as though she'd lived here all her life. Parting ways with this girl was *not* going to be easy.

I could hear Mary Fran and my mother talking downstairs at the front door. Considering what had taken place a few days before, I was none too comfortable to know that Mary Fran was down there talking to my mom. Mary Fran didn't have any idea how clever my mom's sinister interrogation techniques could be. The most hardened communist spies would wither under the grinding pressure of my mother's casual, 'How's it going?'. Mary Fran didn't stand a chance. I decided I'd better hurry up and get downstairs before Mom ended up giving Mary Fran pointers on how best to kiss me.

It seems like whenever you have a bonafide emergency, everything that can possibly go wrong *finds* a way to go wrong. Sneakers not unlacing, jacket zipper getting stuck, play clothes hiding … and all the while, Mom down there, debriefing Mary Fran.

Finally … thankfully … I heard the welcome sound of Eli's voice; a best pal showing up just when I needed him most. His arrival would certainly put a stop to all of that dangerous girl talk.

I hurried down the stairs with the burly little stray right on my tail, and found Eli and Mary Fran in the kitchen, halfway through bologna sandwiches, and eyeballing the tray of cookies that Mom was pulling from the oven.

"Hey! I know that dog!" Eli said, looking past me at my newest best friend.

"Well that was easy," Mom said. "All you guys have to do now is take her home."

"This *is* her home," Eli said with a grin "she was Mr. Hanley's dog."

I could see the look of dread spread across my mom's face and I could almost *hear* her thinking, 'Uh oh' in anticipation of what was coming next. I had to move fast, and make my case before her resolve hardened.

"You *said* we had to find her home and bring her there. Shazam! We *just* did what you said, she's home. You can't send her to the pound now!"

"We don't even know for sure that she was Mr. Hanley's dog," Mom countered.

"Oh, I'm sure ma'am. When I delivered papers for Tommy Peltzer, she chased me down the driveway here every day for two weeks. The one thing she doesn't like is newspapers."

Just then the dog walked over to Mom and sat up in a begging position. That was it! Mom was done, and that was the instant when the stout stray became my dog.

"Alright, alright, she can stay. But she sleeps in the barn."

"What's her name, Eli?" I asked

"I don't know her name, I just know that she runs almost as fast as I can pedal my bike."

"How about Penny then?" I said.

"Penny?" Mom asked quizzically, "why Penny?"

"She's a girl, and she's fast," I explained, "like Penny Cardona, Eli says she's the fastest kid in our class."

CHAPTER TWELVE

The Best of Times
(Told by Josh)

By Saturday, the excitement of the first week of school had faded and school was just school again. With that, we all got back to the more important business of finding Mr. Hanley's treasure. Penny was fitting in just fine as a member of the family. Mom even got over that whole 'sleep in the garage' thing, and Penny was now sleeping on the floor at the foot of my bed. She was up with the sun every morning and Mom would let her outside. That was when she would run off in the general direction of Grout Brook. She was usually gone for about thirty minutes, after which she would come into the house and spend most of the day in the kitchen with mom.

I woke up a bit after eight that Saturday, and Penny was already back from her run and lying in the kitchen by the side door, watching Mom cook breakfast.

"Well, good morning, Sweetie."

"Good morning, Mom."

"What do you have planned for today?"

"We're gonna look for Mr. Hanley's treasure."

"Honey, I think its good that you and your friends have

found an adventure, but I don't want you to get so invested in finding a treasure, that you're disappointed if there is none."

"Don't worry, Mom. We won't be disappointed."

I could tell by her concerned look that she wasn't certain whether I was assuring her that there was a treasure to be found, or promising her that I'd keep my expectations low. Just then, there was a knock and the side door opened. Eli came in right on time, like any good wing man. Mary Fran was right behind him and they stopped at the door.

"Good morning, Mrs. Corey."

"Oh, good morning, Eli, Mary Fran. Come on in."

Penny loved Eli and Mary Fran and she jumped up, tail wagging furiously when they came in. She went right over to Mary Fran, and jumped up and down, paws on Mary Fran's waist.

Mary Fran squatted down and petted her lovingly. "Hey, girl. How you doin' today?"

"Penny, why don't you go home with Mary Fran?" Mom said, smiling and ignoring my disapproving glare.

We started the day by sitting on the front and back porches writing down all of the places we could see that we thought could be landmarks … trees, large boulders, the stone wall. We had about a dozen spots to check and we set about doing so with all of the fervor that one would expect of kids on a treasure hunt. But by two in the afternoon the sun was high, and the day was sweltering. This was summer's last raging stand. After we'd dug, and filled in the last of our fruitless holes, Eli wiped his brow and spoke.

"Let's go swimming."

"Swimming?" I asked. "Who the heck do we know with a pool?"

He looked at me like the city rube that I was. "We don't need a pool, we got Grout Brook."

"It's really clear, pretty water," Mary Fran added.

Dad and I had fished there enough that I knew this. And as I stood there under the blistering rays of the September sun, the idea gained more traction by the moment. It took the three of us about ten minutes to secure all of the required permissions. After that, I went to my room to change while the other two were off to their respective homes to get old sneakers and swimsuits. The plan was to reconvene out at Big Oak; from there we'd ride our bikes along the cut-across path, over to Grout Brook.

The babbling waters of the brook ran crystal clear over the slate bottom and into the aqua colored depths of the deepest hole in the brook. If it was even possible, the gleaming water was clearer and more beautiful than it was the day I fished past sunset with my father. The screech that Mary Fran let out when she stepped into the brook didn't embolden Eli or I at all. Apparently, the water was a bit brisk.

"Well, go on Eli. You're not chicken are you?"

I figured that if I made that pre-emptive accusation, he'd be in no position to shame me into jumping into the obviously frigid water first.

"I'm not chicken," he protested, "I'm just tryin' to decide if I want to jump in or dive."

"I think you're both big sissies!" Mary Fran hollered with a giggle just before she splashed us.

I wish I knew what made girls the way they are. That understanding is a nugget of treasure that men and boys will always seek. But I digress. Back to Grout Brook. After I recovered from the initial shock brought on by Mary Fran's splashing obnoxiousness, I decided that I could either jump in and have fun, or stand on the rocks and bake. I felt the jolt of cold water all the way down to my molars. Then, within a few seconds it didn't feel cold any more. It was the strangest thing. The water had been genuinely cold, but almost immediately, the water felt perfect. It wasn't the normal process of your body getting used to the water, that takes longer. This felt like the water temperature changed to suit me. It was now a welcome relief, and as I looked skyward from beneath the crystal clear water, the blue of the sky seemed more vibrant than I'd ever seen it before. Perhaps the shock to my system kicked my vision into some hyper-acute state that I'd never before experienced. The mix of the scorching sun, the comfortable brook and carefree play with my friends produced the closest thing to drunken revelry that an eleven-year-old could hope to experience.

CHAPTER THIRTEEN

A Sunday Mission
(Told by Josh)

One Sunday we went to 8:00 a.m. church services and as we drove home, Mom asked me if I could get Eli and Mary Fran to come right over. She said she had a job for us. That wasn't likely to be a problem, as the three of us had a standing appointment to spend every spare moment hunting treasure and doing all the other things that kids do.

"Sure Mom. What do you want us to do?"

"I'll tell you when Eli and Mary Fran get to our house," she said, seeming to enjoy keeping me submerged in her little pool of suspense.

There was method to her madness though. When we got home I scrambled to get upstairs, get changed, and go get Eli and Mary Fran. I couldn't stand the suspense and wanted to find out what she had in mind as soon as possible. Within thirty minutes of our car pulling into the driveway, Mary Fran, Eli, and I were all kicking up a trail of dust as we pedaled up the path towards the front of the house where Mom would brief us on our mission.

"You kids hang out by the big oak tree next to the pond all the time, right?"

"Right!" we all said.

"Have you noticed the big patch of blackberries a little bit back from the trail?"

"Sure, Mrs. Corey," Eli said. "They're really getting dark and sweet right now."

"I want to make some pies and I need you kids to pick me some of those berries," Mom explained as she handed me a white cloth sack filled with empty Tupperware style containers.

It went without saying that there would be pie in it for us so I grabbed the sack from Mom, and we raced down from the porch with Penny in hot pursuit. Ten minutes later, we each had a container and were eagerly filling them with wild blackberries. There wasn't a red berry to be found that day. Every berry was dark and bursting with the juicy sweetness infused by a long summer of basking in golden sunshine. As kids will often do, we turned it into a contest, all hurrying to pick the most berries as we giggled and occasionally yelped when an erstwhile thorn nipped at an unguarded patch of flesh. I'm pretty sure the three of us set some sort of record for berry picking that morning. By ten-thirty we were skidding to a stop at the front porch and hurrying our bounty into the kitchen where the smell of three freshly baked pie shells filled the air. We gladly helped rinse our harvest and watched as Mom mixed them into a bowl with cornstarch and various sugars and spices. She heated things on the stove, strained things, mixed things, and finally poured the filling into the waiting pie crusts. Lastly, she sprinkled on crumble toppings and slid the pies into the oven.

It's funny how twenty minutes of waiting for a pie to finish cooking seemed to take an hour longer than twenty minutes spent swimming in Grout Brook. But despite the interminable length of that particular twenty minutes, we three sat on the front porch swing, and we waited … and waited … and waited. The ding of the timer brought us into the kitchen on the run.

"Whoa! Not so fast guys," Mom said, "you kids can have some pie, but first I need you to finish your half of the bargain."

"Finish?" I asked, wondering what further torture we had to endure before we got pie.

We'd have agreed to give a cat a bath if she'd asked us to;

just so long as we got our hands on some of that pie.

"After these pies cool, if I wrap one of them up, can you kids put it in Mary Fran's bicycle basket and ride it into town? This morning at church, I promised Mrs. Devitt that I'd send her a pie today. I'd like you kids to bring it to her. When you get back, you can all have some pie."

"Sure Mom. How long will they take to cool?"

"About forty minutes."

Ugh!

CHAPTER FOURTEEN

Mrs. Devitt
(Told by Josh)

The almost museum-like look and smell of Mrs. Devitt's house brought a flood of memories of my own departed grandmother. Grammy, my last grandparent to die, had passed away when I was seven. While my memories of her were vague, I *distinctly* remembered her house. As a seven-year-old, I had searched every crevice of that house for anything that a little boy might be able to play with, and I'd had precious little success. It wasn't that she begrudged me my fun. Grammy always tried her best to help me find things in her house that I might enjoy playing with.

I recall settling on her large collection of unique salt and pepper shakers. She gladly pulled them all down from the glass-faced cabinets where she kept them on display. There was never any fear that I'd break any of her precious collectibles, just delight at seeing me enjoy my time spent at her house.

Here in Mrs. Devitt's living room, Mary Fran showed a fascination that bordered on awe as she gawked at the ceramic angels that adorned the shelves and cabinets.

"Do you like those?" Mrs. Devitt asked.

Without waiting for an answer, she hobbled over to the cabinet, opened the glass cabinet door, pulled out a chubby little angel figurine and offered it to Mary Fran to hold.

"It's beautiful!" Mary Fran gasped with genuine reverence as she held her hands together to receive the little ceramic cherub.

Mrs. Devitt placed the statuette in Mary Fran's outstretched hands and turned back towards the pie in the kitchen as she spoke.

"Josh, I want you to tell your mother I said thank you for sending me this pie, but I'm an old woman and can't eat a whole pie. Would you kids be willing to help me eat some of it?"

"Well, ma'am, actually when we get back to my house …"

Eli's gentle, but strategically placed kick warned me that I was on the verge of committing a tactical blunder the likes of which hadn't been seen since Goliath took off his helmet to get a better look at David.

I quickly corrected course. "Well … yes, ma'am."

"Then come on in the kitchen," she said without bothering to turn around.

To be honest, I hadn't been very much looking forward to sitting and chatting with an old woman. It wasn't that I had anything against old people. I just didn't know how to talk with them. As it turned out, talking to Mrs. Devitt wasn't much different than talking with Mom or Dad. The most notable difference seemed to be that Mrs. Devitt wasn't at all distracted or too busy to listen to us. Her follow-up questions confirmed her genuine interest in what we thought, and how we felt. It wasn't that Mom and Dad didn't listen or care. It was simply understood that they had everyday responsibilities and concerns that didn't allow them time to sit down and listen to *every* little thing that a kid had to say.

As we all sat, and talked over blackberry pie, an irony crystallized for me. As a person's years fell into precious, short supply, they seemed to have *more* time in their day-to-day lives to listen to the musings and concerns of others, even a bunch of kids.

"So, are you kids enjoying school?" she asked as she refilled mine and Eli's glasses with milk.

Of course, Mary Fran's mouth flew open first. "School is fun. We learn so much new stuff," she said, oblivious to the harsh looks that Eli and I shot her way.

"You boys look like you have a different opinion," Mrs. Devitt observed.

"School's okay," I answered. "It's just that we were working on something else when school started."

"Oh? Can you tell an old lady what you were working on, or is it top secret?"

She probably meant that 'top secret' part as a joke, but I pondered it seriously before I decided that she was probably not a security threat. By then, Eli the frog mouth had beat me to the words.

"We were looking for Mr. Hanley's treasure," he blurted out as soon as he could swallow the pie in his big mouth.

Even though I'd decided it was alright to tell Mrs. Devitt, I was actually quite pleased with the hairy eyeball that Mary Fran shot his way.

"Oh, don't worry kids, your secret is safe with me. A lot of people don't think there ever was a treasure. But I knew him, and I know he was hiding something. Something was definitely troubling him for the last few months of his life."

"You *knew* him?"

"Oh, yes Josh. He was a very kind man. He always gave me a call when he went to the store to see if there was anything I needed. He used to make Jell-O and come over. We'd sit right here at this table and talk about life over a bowl of Jell-O. Sometimes, if he had a good day fishing, he would bring me freshly baked trout. Sure, I've heard the rumors; that there was money from a robbery that happened fifteen years ago. But he was no robber; he was a kind, thoughtful man, not some kind of criminal. I've also heard that there are some plants on his property that have a chemical in them that cures cancer. That one, of course, was also silly. He and I were very close, if he had some magic cure for cancer, he'd have been shoving it down my throat when I had *my* cancer. I think rumors just swirl around quirky people, and he *was* a quirky man."

"Wow!" Mary Fran said, with the glimmer of burgeoning tears in her wide eyes. "My grandma had cancer too, and she died. I wish we had a plant like that when *she* was sick."

"Well, sweetie, remember, that's just a story people were telling," Mrs. Devitt cautioned.

"I know," Mary Fran said fighting back tears. "I just miss my grandma so much."

"I bet you were a wonderful granddaughter." Mrs. Devitt rubbed Mary Fran's back and gave her a hug that *I* could feel from where I was sitting. "I wish I had a granddaughter like you. I wasn't lucky enough to have any grandchildren."

CHAPTER FIFTEEN

A Summer Storm
(Told by Josh)

The air was thick with the smell of the coming storm as we started back home from Mrs. Devitt's house. It's not that we wouldn't have raced to see who could get there first anyway, but the ominous clouds added another level of urgency. The leaves turned pale-side-up as the moisture-laden wind picked up in intensity. You could smell the rainstorm brewing in the air. We had another quarter-mile to go when the first huge raindrops began falling. We screeched with delight as we pedaled up the road through what was becoming a driving rain. Our squeals brought Penny to the end of the driveway on the run, where she waited patiently to meet us with a manically wagging tail, seemingly oblivious to the downpour.

We were all soaked by the time we got off our bikes and scampered beneath the shelter of the front porch, where Mom met us with three towels.

"Well, you guys finally got back. I was beginning to worry."

"Sorry, Mom. We got to talking with Mrs. Devitt and we lost track of time."

"Wow, first Amy at the library, now Mrs. Devitt. You kids are spending a lot of time talking to grownups lately. I'm a little jealous." She handed a towel to each of us.

"She's *really* nice. She was telling us all about Mr. Hanley."

"Really? She knew Mr. Hanley?"

"Yeah, Mom, they were friends. Mr. Hanley used to pick up stuff from the market for her and they used to sit and talk. She said that Mr. Hanley used to bring her Jell-o and baked trout, and he was a very nice man."

"Gee, maybe she can give you some information to help with your treasure hunt," Mom said, walking back inside the house. "I'll bring out some milk for you kids."

Fifteen minutes later, we all sat on the porch swing breathing in that delightful aroma that always accompanies a heavy rain, and laughing uncontrollably at Penny as she darted out from beneath the shelter of the porch and ran jubilantly through the driving torrent. She'd leap joyfully skyward, gulping at the falling rain, then turn and bolt for the cover of the porch. On the porch, she would get as close as she could to all three of us and shake herself dry bringing giggles and shrieks of glee.

When Penny finally settled down, she stretched out on the porch and watched us all huddle in our respective towels as we drank milk and swung beneath the fierce pattering of raindrops on the porch roof.

"What if the treasure ends up being a hundred dollars for each of us? What will you guys do with your share?"

"I don't know, Josh," Eli said, "maybe I'd get my Mom an electric blanket. She works hard, and she's always so tired when the end of the day comes."

"Well, I'd get a fancy new red dress, and save the rest of my share for college."

"A dress?" I asked. "Why would you get a new dress? I hardly *ever* see you wearing a dress."

"Sometimes a girl just wants to look pretty," she answered with a sigh and a roll of her eyes.

"I might not get anything. I just like the idea of being the guy to find a treasure. I always hear about people who are lookin'

59

for treasure, but nobody ever finds any. I just wanna be the guy who looks for treasure and actually *finds* it."

"You never hear about people finding treasure," Mary Fran said, looking at me like I was a pathetic boob, "because when people *find* treasure, they keep their mouths shut about it, so nobody comes to try and take it from them."

Almost on cue, the rain stopped, the sun cut the clouds, and the most brilliant rainbow arched across the sky.

CHAPTER SIXTEEN

Bus Brawl
(Told by Josh)

The trouble erupted on Monday's bus ride home while the three of us were sitting together in adjacent seats. We were talking about what we were going to do that night. As usual, I was the one doing all of the talking, and Mary Fran and Eli were listening. I told them that we'd all meet with our bikes at my house as fast as they could get changed and get there. But Mary Fran wasn't listening. Only after the fact, did it occur to me that she hadn't been looking at me as I spoke, but looking past me. She was focused about four seats ahead of me, where Derrick Kearny was menacing a very small, very alone boy.

Now, Derrick Kearny was a well-known goon in school. In case you are unfamiliar with the science of goonology, goons are never small. Derrick was tall, like Eli, but he was *not* skinny like Eli. Derrick looked like he was an inflatable raft and someone had pulled the ripcord.

Under normal circumstances, Eli and I would never have gotten into a fracas with him. But Mary Fran didn't leave us any choice. Stupid girls! Derrick lunged toward the smaller boy and in an instant, the protective instinct in Mary Fran must have kicked in. She shot from her seat, past me and in one flying leap, covered the distance between herself, and the stunned Derrick Kearny. He went sprawling down the aisle on impact. For just a moment, Eli and I snickered. But when Derrick got up, the look on his face told us we had to get involved. His flabby cheeks went beet red, his porcine nostrils flared, and his eyes burned. Somehow, Eli and I managed to storm past Mary Fran and into the path of the raging bully. He was throwing punches that had no particular target, yet somehow, one of them found my left eye. Despite my throbbing eye, between the two of us, Eli and I managed to pin Derrick to the floor before the boy who'd been his original target and Mary Fran jumped on top of the whole dog pile. It felt like an eternity passed before the brakes whined and the school bus slowed to a stop.

Mrs. White was a kindly old bus driver, but on that day I learned that one did not want to find one's self on her bad side. After pulling Mickey and Mary Fran from the scrum, she jerked Eli and I from atop Derrick by our collars and questioned bystanders to determine what and who had started the disruption.

Fortunately, the other kids on the bus recalled that things had happened in much the same way as the four of us told the story. They confirmed that Derrick was the aggressor and that the three of us had merely been sticking up for the smaller boy. Mrs. White escorted Derrick, by ear, to the seat directly behind her and carried on with her appointed rounds. That's when Mary Fran introduced us all to Mickey. It turns out that he lived a quarter mile out past Mary Fran with his parents, his grandmother, and his two older sisters. Of course, since we all got off the bus before Mickey, he already had a rough idea where we lived, or at least that we all got off at Eli's house.

As we neared our stop, despite my throbbing eye, I began to feel good about jumping in and sticking up for Mary Fran and Mickey. It felt like we'd done the right thing.

"Hey Mickey, we're all going to Josh's to go swimming in the creek, you wanna come over with us?" Eli asked.

"Sure. I gotta do some chores first though," Mickey said, smiling for the first time I could recall.

"Can you meet Mary Fran and me at my house in thirty minutes?" Eli asked. "That's the house where we all get off the bus."

"Sure, Eli. But I might be about forty minutes. Can you wait for me?"

"We won't leave without you," Mary Fran assured him just as the bus came to our stop and the three of us got up. "That's Eli's house down that driveway," she said as she pointed. "We'll wait for you on the back porch."

"I'll hurry," Mickey said, as the three of us piled off the bus, each shooting a cross-ways glare at Derrick as we passed him.

When I came inside, Mom's reaction was exactly as I'd expected it to be.

"Oh my God, Sweetheart! What happened to your eye?" she shrieked as if it were dangling out of the socket.

"Mary Fran started a fight on the bus and me and Eli had to jump in to make sure she didn't get killed."

"Oh stop," Mom said, already wrapping ice cubes in a dish towel. "Mary Fran is such a sweet little girl. I refuse to believe that she would start a fight."

"Tell that to Derrick Kearny! She dropped him like a bag of dirt! And he smacked his head on the back of a seat on his way down too."

As I recounted the story, the truth of my words really began to sink in. She tackled that big oaf with picture-perfect form -- head down, low center of gravity, and shoulders square. Mom must have seen the amusement on my face.

"Well, there is nothing funny about fighting young man! Why did Mary Fran start a fight? What happened?"

I put Mom's improvised ice pack on my eye as I explained what happened from the beginning, from Kearny picking on Mickey, all the way to the end. I could see the softening wash across Mom's face as I told the story. By the time I got to the part about Mary Fran's tackling form, which I included mostly for my own amusement, Mom was struggling to suppress a grin herself. Looking back on that day, I now understand why Mom never played poker.

"Well, standing up for someone smaller is a good thing, but you know how your father and I feel about fighting!" she said, trying her best to sound stern. "I'm not going to punish you, but I won't run interference for you with your father. You're on your own there."

Just then, Penny ran to the window. She jumped up, put her paws on the window sill with her tail wagging furiously, and barked a couple of times. It was Eli, Mary Fran, and Mickey. They came bursting through the door in that order, each trying to elbow their way in first.

"Oh, Mary Fran! Sweetheart, what did that boy do to you? Are you alright?" Mom asked as she turned Mary Fran every which way, checking for any marks, while I stood, holding an improvised ice pack on my eye.

"I'm fine, Mrs. Corey. Josh and Eli protected me." Mary Fran threw a peculiar look my way.

"You're not fine. Look at your knee, you're bleeding!"

Mary Fran looked down and was pretty nonchalant about it.

"Oh yeah, I think I banged my knee on the floor of the bus when I tackled Derrick. It looks worse than it is. My mom put a bandage on it but bandages don't stay on knees very good. I guess it fell off while I was riding my bike over here."

Mom didn't seem to care that Mary Fran's wound had already been tended to. She went into immediate action, getting out a tube of disinfectant, tearing paper towels off the roll, and running some of them under hot water. Mary Fran protested that her mom had already cleaned it, but to no avail. She winced as Mom cleaned her knee with wet paper towels.

"And you must be Mickey!" Mom said, now applying the second layer of disinfectant that Mary Fran's knee had received in the last ten minutes.

"Yes, ma'am, Michael Thomas Booth, but everybody calls me Mickey."

"Are you okay? I heard you were in the fight too," she said, still holding the paper towel and the tube of disinfectant.

I rolled my eyes. Yeah Mom, everyone with two good eyes is okay.

Mickey nodded and Mom put away her medical supplies and quit fawning over everyone else. Well, almost. She was going to bandage Mary Fran's knee again, but Mary Fran talked her down. She explained that we were going swimming and the bandage would just fall off again anyway. It was almost as though she'd heard my thoughts. Sometimes I wonder about that.

"Okay, you kids go wash your hands, and I'll make you something to eat."

Since only three of us could fit in the tiny downstairs bathroom, I figured I'd change into some shorts and wash my hands in the upstairs bathroom.

"I'm gonna go upstairs and change my clothes Mom, I'll be downstairs in a few minutes," I shouted back over my shoulder as I went upstairs.

Of course, Penny was right on my heels all the way into my room, and she kept a close watch on me while I got changed. "Hey, Penny," I said as I scratched her head enthusiastically, "have you been a good girl today? I'll pet you some more later. I gotta go now."

I hurried into the bathroom and washed my hands and my face. When I pulled the towel down from drying my face, there she was standing in the door with Penny.

"Mary Fran! What are you doing up here?"

She'd never been upstairs in my house before, so to say I was a bit startled would be the biggest understatement since General Custer said 'I think there might be a few Indians over that next ridge.'

She took a step closer to me. I was only half a foot, but it felt like she stepped between me and my skin. I backed up.

She took another step closer. "I wanted to talk to you in private."

"What about?"

"About Mickey."

I stepped back. "What about him?"

"He's a really nice kid," she said, "but he's so shy."

"Yeah?"

"Well, I want us to count him in on the treasure." Based on what she said next, I figure I must have given her a look. "If you don't wanna cut the treasure into four parts, he can have my share. I just want to include him. He doesn't have a lot of friends."

She stepped in closer again and I tried to back up, but I

65

backed into the sink and couldn't go any farther. "Okay, okay. He's in. We'll cut the treasure four ways!"

"Oh thank you Josh! Thank you. You're so sweet."

Then she got that crazy look on her face and she did it again! Before I could defend myself, she leaned in and planted another kiss on me. She got me flush on the lips this time. Then she giggled one of those stupid girl-giggles, and before I knew it she was gone. She was halfway down the stairs before I could pry myself from my slack-jawed stupor.

CHAPTER SEVENTEEN

The Deep Hole
(Told by Josh)

I didn't think it was possible, but that day Grout Brook was more crystal clear than I'd ever seen it. Maybe it was the brilliant sun that day, or maybe the water was just that much clearer, but it was no illusion. When I cannonballed into the deep hole, I was surprised. We'd had enough cold nights since the last time we went swimming, that I expected to come up with blue lips. But the stream was incredibly comfortable, just as it had been before. When I opened my eyes underwater, a whole new world appeared before me. Sunbeams reached into the pool like the fingers of God, and I could see how remarkably deep this hole was. It was, in fact, bottomless, at least in one spot. At the bottom of this pool was the opening to an underwater cave, as wide as the opening of a two-car garage. We'd had trouble touching bottom with our fishing lures there, but I assumed it was just a very deep spot. This explained where all of these remarkably large trout were coming from. I watched trout as fat as watermelons glide through the sparkling depths with flicks of their huge tails. The rainbow trout had brilliant red stripes running the length of their sides. The brown trout had gill covers that were just as red, with bodies covered in dark spots, even their fins. The brook trout were the smallest ones, but they were not small. They were distinguished by slightly darker bodies with light spots and very faint vertical bars. Bright white stripes ran along the edges of all of their fins. It was like white trim. I was dumbstruck. I saw now, that the fish Dad and I had been catching, and thought were so big, were the small ones. The big ones were bigger around than phone poles, and some were easily three feet long. They rarely ventured out of that underwater cave. They were bigger than any trout I'd ever seen. I had never even *imagined* that trout could get that big.

"Holy cow! Did you see those trout?" Eli yelled when we popped up for air.

"Shhhhh," I demanded, finger to lips. "You want everybody to come sneaking in on our stream and ruin the fishing?"

Then Mickey and Mary Fran popped up.

"Wow! This water feels great," Mickey said. "I thought it would be cold."

"Those trout are huge," Mary Fran added. "I bet some of them are world records."

"*Shut up!* You're gonna have the whole world out here."

"Relax, Josh," she said, "this is your property all around us. Who's gonna hear us? There's not another person for a hundred yards.

"Geez," Eli said, "I thought he was full of it when he was telling us about all those big trout that him and his dad caught out here."

I, of course, gave him the most disdainful side-eye in my arsenal. I was going to set that carrot-topped leprechaun straight, but Mary Fran was faster with a reprimand.

"Eli, it looks like you owe Josh an apology."

"I guess I do. Sorry, Josh, I thought you had a screw loose or something."

"What kind of trout are they?" Mickey asked.

"Me and Dad caught brown trout, but I think there were other kinds down there. Let me go down and have another look."

I went under, re-surfaced, and grabbed a quick breath. "Looks like there's browns, rainbows, and brookies down there, and there's a bunch of them."

"You know," Mickey said, "if there really is a world record fish down there, I saw a TV show that said that world record fish are worth a lot of money to whoever catches them."

Mary Fran, Eli, and I exchanged the same looks, all with the same thought hidden behind them.

Could these trout be the treasure?

Nobody said anything because Mickey hadn't officially been cut in yet. The treasure hunting cabal was still only a trio.

"Hey! You know what we ought to do? We ought to swim down there and explore that cave."

Mary Fran looked at Eli like he'd just passed gas in church. "Did you hit your fool head in that scuffle with Derrick? We could *die* in an underwater cave like that."

"Yeah," Mickey said, "if my folks knew that cave was under there, I bet they wouldn't even let me come swimming over here."

"Mickey's right," I said. "We probably shouldn't say anything to our parents about this."

After another hour in the water, we decided we'd better head on home. It took a lot of convincing, and promises that none of us would ever go in that cave, but we got Mary Fran to agree not to tell the grown-ups that it was down there. We hopped on our bikes and started the ride back to my house.

I don't know why it is, but it seems like you're always at least halfway to wherever you're going when you realize you forgot something and you have to go back. This time, we were way more than halfway home when we realized there was a problem.

Mary Fran skidded to a stop. "We have to go back!"

"What?" I groaned. "What for?"

"I forgot my bracelet. I took it off and put it on a rock so I wouldn't lose it in the water."

"Oh for Pete's sake! For somebody so smart, that was pretty dumb."

"I gotta admit," she said, "you're right." It felt good to hear her say I was right and my chest was just starting to puff out when she dropped the other shoe, right on my head. "And if there's one thing boys are experts on, it's stupid."

Eli and Mickey were on the ground, seized by spasms of laughter until I reminded them that they were also boys, the knuckleheads!

When we caught up to Mary Fran, she was stopped thirty yards from the water with her hand held out behind her, giving us a 'stop' signal. She was looking up the trail at the deep hole as I rolled up next to her and saw what she was looking at. There was a lady swimming naked in the hole. She looked like she was a little bit older than Amy, from the library, but her hair was blonde and longer than Amy's. It went halfway down her back. Eli and Mickey rolled up next, and they came up with the same brilliant, commentary.

"Wow!"

Mickey elaborated. "Who's *that*?"

While we boys were paralyzed in a state of slack-jawed amazement, Mary Fran seemed remarkably unfazed.

"Oh great," she whispered. "How am I gonna get my bracelet now?"

"I'll get it," Mickey said, and before we could stop him, he hopped off his bike and disappeared into the bushes.

Two minutes later, I pried my eyes off of that magnificent, naked lady to see a little hand slip out of the bushes by the rock and pick up Mary Fran's bracelet. Shortly after that, we were on our way to my house.

CHAPTER EIGHTEEN

Amy's Story
(Told by Amy)

The library was empty and I was bored, so I decided to get ahead on the next day's work. I went outside to collect the returned books from the drop box and was re-shelving them when one of them caught my eye. It was a copy of Robert Louis Stevenson's *Treasure Island*. The word 'treasure' reminded me of the kids who'd been asking about treasure at the old Hanley farm. Josh Corey's family had recently moved into the place, and he and his two friends, Eli and Mary Fran, were mesmerized by the possibility of finding hidden treasure somewhere on the property. The hopes of those adorable kids both nagged at me and delighted me until I decided to do a little research for them. I thought perhaps I could help them, or at least add to the adventure of their quest. To my way of thinking, the only treasure was those three young minds, and I figured if I helped them, maybe I could get myself three library patrons for life. With that in mind, I decided to nose around a bit.

Figuring I would start with the basics, I went to the computer that had the index for the local newspaper, opened the search function, and keyed in 'Caleb Hanley'. After a few seconds,

71

the results popped up in the familiar green text. These results displayed every edition and page of *The Daily Standard* that included the name 'Caleb Hanley'. The most recent entry was on the top. As expected, that entry was dated May 15, 1983, one week after Hanley was killed. It was a story about his murder. The preceding entries included one in the death notices, one in the obituaries, and several more stories about his murder. After that, Mr. Hanley's name appeared in news entries that were typical for a rural farmer. There were a couple of feature stories about farming and four entries announcing the winners of awards at the county fair. There was a news piece about an automobile accident in which a drunk driver had struck Hanley's car, and then things got weird.

The story about his murder indicated that Caleb Hanley died at the age of forty-five. This, and a bit of quick math, told me that I should see Hanley's birth announcement somewhere around 1939. What I found instead, was a story about a forty-five-year-old Caleb Hanley having saved a woman and two children from a burning house on December 8, 1937. Had Mr. Hanley been forty-five years old for the last forty-six years, or was something amiss in the archives of *The Daily Standard*?

Searching down the screen, I found several more entries, referring to minor news stories about more farming and county fair awards. They were clearly too old to be about *our* Caleb Hanley. Finally, I found a birth record for a Caleb Hanley, but the date was November 22, 1839. Could our Mr. Hanley have been Caleb Hanley Jr.? No, the math still wasn't right. If our Caleb Hanley, who died at 45, was Caleb Hanley Jr., and this birth record was for Caleb Hanley Sr., he would had to have been ninety-nine years old when he became a father – highly unlikely. It was possible that our Caleb Hanley was Caleb Hanley III, but what were the odds that the birth records for both Caleb Hanley Jr., *and* Caleb Hanley III, would be lost?

Being a rural, small-town library in 1984, we frequently received requests for help researching family trees. As a result, I often found myself contacting Hillary Shea. Hillary, the village clerk, had become a good friend, and my main resource for researching birth certificates, marriage licenses, property transfers, and death certificates. When I called her, I explained that the newspapers didn't have complete information on Caleb Hanley of 1460 DeLeon Road, and asked her if she could see what she could find out. She called me back in less than ten minutes.

"Hey, Amy, it's me, Hillary."

"Hi, Hillary. Were you able to find anything?"

"Oh yeah", she said a tad dramatically, "I checked the birth records first. A Caleb Hanley was born to Jacob and Anna Hanley on September 27, 1839, in the farmhouse at 1460 DeLeon Road. This was the only birth record that the village had on file for anyone named Caleb Hanley. I checked property tax records next and there was nothing earth-shattering there. There were annual tax assessments and the Federal farm credit, but these records don't always have the property owner's name on them since they're property specific."

"Okay."

"One thing I noticed in the tax assessments ..."

"I'm all ears."

"The tax assessment was just about the minimum assessment from 1942 to 1945. Now that's not unusual. During World War II, if a farmer went away to war and there was no one to work his farm, the state and county gave him a substantial tax break. It wouldn't do to have someone go to war to defend his country, and come home to find out the county or state has seized his farm."

I thought about that Screaming Eagles patch the kids had brought me, but I kept that to myself. "So how is that significant then?"

"Well, it tells us that the man of the house was of age to be sent off to war, *and* didn't have a son old enough to work the farm in his absence."

"Now, things got interesting when I checked the property transactions." For me, things had already become interesting, but I let Hillary continue. "The property was deeded to Jacob Hanley on August 15, 1838 through the Farm Act of 1838. This record isn't remarkable at all. This was when the deeds to most of the farms in this area were first granted. The interesting part is that there were only three other transactions for this property, the first when the farm was transferred to Caleb Hanley in 1856. There's also a death notice for Jacob Hanley in 1856, so that fits. After that, there's a record for when the county assumed ownership, and one when the Corey's bought it from the county. Those last two transactions both occurred that year, 1984, which means, according to the records, no transactions have occurred between 1857 and 1984. That's a hundred and twenty-seven years, and according to every document I have, the Caleb Hanley who died in 1984 was the same Caleb Hanley who acquired the farm in 1856."

My jaw dropped and hung slack. "Are you kidding me?"

"I don't have records of any other Caleb Hanley's being born, registering for school, marrying, having children, or purchasing land … nothing at all."

"Hillary, that's crazy. Someone *must* have failed to enter a transaction. The only other explanation would be that Hanley was almost a hundred and forty-five when he died."

"Well, based on his photo in the paper, he was a very well-preserved, very, very old man."

We shared a laugh, and Hillary said she'd do a bit more investigating and would let me know what she found out in a few days. This troubled me for the rest of that day. What were the chances of property transaction records, birth records, *and* death records all being missing for the same person? Something was very peculiar.

CHAPTER NINETEEN

The Duck's Head Buck
(Told by Josh)

We made it back to my house forty minutes before it got dark. That meant we had about twenty-five minutes before the others had to head for home. Our plan was to use those twenty-five minutes to go through the boxes of Mr. Hanley's pictures and documents. We didn't expect to find anything important. The reality was that this was nothing more than an excuse for a bunch of kids to hang out with each other a little bit longer.

Since Dad usually stayed out working until dark so he could get as much done as possible, late dinners were common. Accordingly, Mom was in the kitchen cooking dinner and gave me her typical sideways glance when I came in ahead of my three friends.

"Well, it's about time you guys got back. Did you have a nice time?"

"It was great, Mom," I said, moving aside to untie my sneakers while letting the others in, "you wouldn't believe how clear the water was."

"That's nice," she said, straining hot water off a pan of potatoes, still eyeballing the four of us. "Are you hungry?"

"You bet," I said. "When do we eat?"

That was when mom saw it. "Mary Fran, your knee!"

This of course, led us all to look at her knee. Everyone but Eli saw what Mom saw and immediately understood the significance.

"What?" Eli asked, staring at Mary Fran's knee, and trying to see what everyone else saw.

For her part, Mary Fran was speechless, staring in stunned silence at her now undamaged knee.

"Are you sure your knee was hurt?" Mom asked, "Could you have had someone else's blood on your knee?"

I rolled my eyes. "Mom, you cleaned her knee yourself."

Mom's look turned timid, as if she was questioning her own sanity.

"I don't know," Mary Fran said, with a startled look on her face. "All I know is my knee *did* hurt and it doesn't hurt anymore."

"Oh, well, okay then," Mom said, rubbing the outside of her left arm with her right hand. "Are you kids sure you won't stay for dinner?"

"No thank you," the three of them said all at once.

"Me and Mickey have a math test tomorrow," Mary Fran said. Mickey nodded in agreement.

"My mom said I need to eat at home," Eli said. "She says if I eat here too much more, my folks will have to let you claim me on your taxes."

Mom smiled as we kids headed for the basement stairs, but I knew that arm rubbing gesture of hers. Something was bothering her. It was obvious that Mary Fran was pretty rattled too. She kept touching her knee as we all went down to the basement. I took everybody into the corner, where I'd put all of Mr. Hanley's things and we each took a box. I'd been through these boxes before, but I figured it didn't hurt to look again. Besides, like I said before, it was also an excuse for my friends to come over.

Apparently, Mr. Hanley was a bit of an outdoorsman, because my box had mostly nature pictures, photographic records of his outdoor adventures, and those of his ancestors from decades before. There was a thick stack of pictures of Mr. Hanley, out at

Grout Brook showing off various trout, many of which were every bit as big as the ones that Dad and I had been catching. There were also decades of photos of birds, deer, bears and other wildlife. Because I loved fishing, I was drawn to the photos of the trout, and as a young boy, I was equally drawn to the pictures of bears. Eli was sitting next to me, and he had more hunting and fishing pictures. Mickey and Mary Fran were going through boxes that were filled mostly with family pictures.

Eli elbowed me to show me an old photo. "Look at this buck's pattern."

"Oh yeah," I said, taking the picture, "my dad told me about deer like that. He has some albino genes that give him those patches of white in his coat. They're called Piebold or Piebald or something like that."

Mickey's head jerked up from the photos he was looking at. "Hey, can I see it?" he asked with an outstretched hand.

I gave him the picture and went back to going through my stack of photos while he and Mary Fran looked at the buck.

"He's beautiful," Mary Fran said.

"I've seen this deer," Mickey said. "He's been coming around our cornfield, by where the woods come up to our house."

Mary Fran smiled and took the picture from him. "I don't think *that* deer has been coming around your field, Mickey. See how that picture isn't color or black and white? See how it's in shades of reddish-brown?"

Mickey nodded. "Yeah?"

"That's called sepia. That's the way all photos looked in the eighteen hundreds and early nineteen hundreds."

Me and Eli looked at each other with what was becoming an all too common expression. *How the heck does she know all this stuff?* I mean, I knew a lot of old pictures were in those rust-colored shades, but I had no idea what it was called, or exactly *how* old they were.

"I'm telling you!" Mickey insisted, "I have seen *that* deer in our cornfield. See that splotch of white on his side that's shaped like a duck's head? The deer I see by my house has that *same* splotch of white."

The rest of us shared a glance and an eye-roll, and Mary

Fran said what we were all thinking. "Okay, Mickey."

Eventually, Eli and Mickey were summoned home, and I was uneasy about having been left alone in the basement with an 'ambush kisser'.

"Hey Josh," she said, "come look at this."

My stomach churned. Was this a trick? Was she going to nail me again? Did I want her to plant one on me or not? I got up, cautiously walked over to where she sat, stopped two or three feet away, but didn't sit down.

"Yeah?"

"Does the woman in this picture remind you of anybody?"

She did *not* remind me of anyone, at least not on a conscious level.

CHAPTER TWENTY

Mary Fran's Story
(Told by Mary Fran)

Josh, Eli and Mickey saw nothing that day but the naked lady. I remember that day as if it was yesterday. The water in Grout Brook was normally pretty clear, but on *that* day the water was even more clear than usual. The boys might not have seen it right away, but for me, the events of that day were what began to bring the reality of the treasure into sharper focus.

We'd been swimming down at the brook when the remarkable clarity of the water revealed incredible things. No, I'm not talking about the blonde lady's tan. What I'm talking about is the bread crumbs, the clues to where we should have been looking for the treasure. The crystal clear waters of Grout Brook revealed a hole in the creek bed. I'm talking about a real hole, an opening in the shale creek bed that led into what could only be described as an underwater cave. At first, I was afraid to swim over the opening, fearing that there could be some kind of whirlpool or suction that might pull me into that watery abyss. But my curiosity proved to be greater than my fear. Emboldened by this curiosity, I swam just three feet over the opening and peered into the darkness. Other than the schools of large minnows and the huge trout that hunted, and sometimes ate them, I couldn't see a thing, no walls, no bottom, nothing. The other thing I noticed was that the water around the opening was warm. In fact, I had the idea that the opening was keeping the rest of the hole warmer than a clear spring-fed stream should be.

While I was busy noticing all of that, what I was *not* noticing, was that at some point between jumping into the creek and drying myself off, my knee had healed. I'm not speaking metaphorically. My knee ... *healed.* When I bent it to get off that school bus, that knee throbbed like it had its own heartbeat. The pain had literally been pulsing through it, but I was determined not to let it show. I didn't want the boys to think I wasn't tough.

I played dumb when Mrs. Corey asked about my knee because I had promised the boys I would keep quiet about our treasure hunt. I pretended I hadn't noticed, but I noticed.

In fact, the reason I forgot my bracelet was that when we got out of the water and were drying off, I noticed that the cut was gone. To say I was bothered by this wouldn't exactly be accurate. I was, of course, happy that it had stopped hurting. But at the same time, I was perplexed by what had happened. As much as I enjoyed silently mocking the boys for their intellectual shortcomings, I was so bedeviled by my miraculously healed knee, that I forgot my bracelet. Worse yet, just like the boys, I overlooked the obvious.

At the time, I didn't understand the effect that a beautiful, naked woman had over anyone with a Y chromosome, otherwise known as males. A tyrannosaurus-rex could have walked out of Grout Brook, got on one of their bikes, and pedaled off into the sunset, and none of them would have noticed a thing. This is why the male of the species cannot be asked to recall anything about the face of a woman he's just seen naked. I'd seen on TV that the police interview witnesses to a crime separately, so that what one person says doesn't influence the memory of another. With that in mind, I asked the boys separately if the woman we saw at Grout Brook reminded them of anyone. True to form, when I showed them the photograph, none of the boys saw any resemblance.

The old sepia photograph was taken in town. The blonde woman was posing on the hood of a 1908 Model T parked in front of a business whose storefront sign identified it as Granger's Drug Store and Soda Fountain. When none of the boys recognized her, I questioned myself. Maybe I was seeing things. Maybe the woman in the picture *wasn't* a dead ringer for the woman we'd seen naked at Grout Brook. But two days later, while I was grocery shopping with my mom, I saw and recognized the woman for the third time. My mother knew her, she addressed her by name. She called her Aggie.

In the car, on the way home, I asked my mom who the woman she spoke to was. My mother's answer ignited an explosion of revelation. Aggie was Agnes Granger and had been the fiance of the late Caleb Hanley. I immediately made the connection between her last name and the name of the drug store in the old photograph that I'd seen in Josh's basement. That explained how she even knew that particular deep hole existed, that it was there, in the middle of the Corey's property. I thought about my knee and wondered. Who was Agnes Granger? Would she be at all surprised to know how the waters of Grout Brook seemed to have healed my knee?

"Where do you know her from?" I asked.

"She works down at the pharmacy."

Boom! Grangers Pharmacy, old picture, my knee? Boom again! Josh Corey lived on DeLeon Road. Could it be? Could that really be what the treasure was? This was madness, and I tried to shake it out of my head, but it had already stuck. How was I going to tell the boys what I suspected without having them think I was nuts?

CHAPTER TWENTY-ONE

Saving Face
(Told by Josh)

Thursday at the bus stop, when Mary Fran pulled me aside, I caught the flicker of a jealous scowl on Eli's face.

"Hey Josh," she whispered, "I think I found the treasure."

I imagine my brow furrowed like the sides of an accordion at that moment because I was thinking that she'd gone completely batty. How the heck had *she* cracked the code? How had *she* found the secret of the Hanley treasure this fast, all by herself?

"What?"

"I think I know what the treasure is!"

"Well, why'd you pull me over here, away from Eli?"

"I didn't want everybody to think I was a crackpot."

I tried to beat it back, but a smirk slipped across my lips. *Well, that horse has already left the barn.*

"What makes you think I won't tell Eli, and we won't be making fun of you in three minutes?"

She looked down the road to see if the bus was coming yet. "Well, I'm telling you anyways. I figured it out, and if you'd just hush up and *listen* for a minute -"

"Hey Eli," I yelled, "come over here."

By the look on his face, he was very happy, and maybe a little relieved that I called him and he hurried over.

"Go ahead, Mary Fran, tell Eli what you told me."

She gave me a quick glare, looked down the road again, then spoke up. "Well ... I think I know what the treasure is!"

"Oh yeah?" Eli said excitedly. "What is it? Where is it?"

Eli didn't laugh at Mary Fran, he didn't furrow his brow like I had. He didn't even roll his eyes. I was so disappointed in him. What a schnook!

"I think the treasure is Grout Brook."

"What?"

"If you'd be quiet and listen -"

"Okay, okay, go ahead and talk."

"I think it's the *water*. My knee had a pretty bad cut, and it was hurting something awful, but after we went swimming in Grout Brook, it didn't hurt anymore. And look at your eye! It's all better too."

I touched my eye. I couldn't even remember when it stopped hurting. With all the fuss over Mary Fran's knee, I hadn't paid attention. All of this was enough to make me let go of some of my doubts for a moment. I thought about the big blue bottles of water in our cellar. I'd seen jugs like that in offices before, and had just assumed that Mr. Hanley didn't like the well water. Or maybe they kept that water in the basement for when the power went out. But we had a storm take the power out once, and the water kept running. Our house was connected to the town water supply, and the water tasted just fine.

I remembered something else that had happened in our first week in the house. What no one else knew, what had bothered me since Mary Fran's knee episode, was that I'd scratched my leg pretty bad while playing in the barn. The next day, I went fishing with Dad, I waded into the stream and had the exact same healing experience.

As I thought about that, I was chastened. My attitude had undergone a complete turn around in a matter of minutes.

"We should test it one more time," I said.

Eli made one thing abundantly clear. "Well don't look at me! I'm not cutting myself to test your dumb idea."

Since Mary Fran always liked to demonstrate how much smarter than us she was, I expected her to come up with some sort of plan to test this theory. But going by her distant stare, she was someplace far, far away. It turns out, that place was a quarter-mile up Nichols Corners Road, where it met DeLeon Road. Mary Fran had heard the diesel roar of the school bus before we had. She could even hear better than we could.

By the time the school day ended and we got on the bus for the trip home, fate and a tree root at school had conspired to give us our test subject.

"God, *look* at that shiner! What happened to you Eli?"

"Hey there, Josh. Oh, I tripped on a tree root out in the playground and fell on my face."

"Man," Mickey said, "that had to hurt."

Mary Fran cringed at Eli's blackened eye and the big red scratch on the side of his face. But then her expression jumped from that pained look to a smile. She said exactly what I was thinking.

"It looks like we have our volunteer to uhm … test the waters." She was grinning like she was the first person to ever make a pun, but I refused to smile so she went on. "And this time we're gonna take before and after pictures. Eli, you come to my house, we'll take a picture of your face with my camera. You can call your mom from there and ask her if you can stay for a while. Tell her I'm helping you with your homework."

Eli nodded. "Okay."

Mary Fran turned to me next. "Josh, you and Mickey go get changed to go swimming, and be sure you bring a pair of shorts and a towel for Eli, and some old sneakers if you got any."

We all went swimming at the brook for about an hour, and as much as I tried to just enjoy an afternoon of swimming, I couldn't help keeping an eye on Eli's face, and I watched it happen. When Eli dried off and got back into his own clothes, I knew one more thing about Grout Brook. Besides having *extraordinarily* large trout, Grout Brook's waters *were* healing waters. I wondered if these two things were related and decided that I would ask Amy about this on Saturday when I went down to the library. Amy had shown the willingness to listen to us and was the adult least likely to think I was just a nutty kid.

CHAPTER TWENTY-TWO

Miracle Elixir
(Told by Josh)

As I stood on the shore of Grout Brook, fishing pole in hand, the first sliver of golden sun broke the Saturday morning horizon. Though I enjoyed fishing, on that day it was the sparkling waters of Grout Brook that had drawn me. As the sun crept higher, I tied on a number three, dressed Mepps Aglia spinner and made several mindless casts to the top of the deep hole, retrieving the lure across the creek as the current swept it downstream. I was thinking about the library and the waters at my feet more than I was thinking about catching any of its inhabitants. I couldn't wait to tell Amy about our suspicions regarding the stream. Unfortunately, since the library didn't open until 9:30 on Saturday mornings, I had two and a half hours to kill. On my third cast, a hard thump doubled my fishing rod over. The drag on my reel squealed, and there was a bathtub-sized boil at the surface. My rod snapped back up to straight and the fight was over, just like that. I muttered a word that wasn't allowed across my lips and reeled in empty fishing line, no trout, no Mepps spinner, no nothing.

I'd actually gone there to be close to Grout Brook and to think. I brought the fishing pole and small tackle box out of habit.

Since I wasn't really there for the fishing, I didn't bother tying on another spinner. I just leaned my pole against a tree, sat on a big rock next to the gurgling stream and thought. If these were healing waters, I reasoned, it was so weird that they could have led to Mr. Hanley's death? I wondered, if this was the treasure, was there some way it could make us rich? Eventually, I drifted off into that 'free mind' state, in which a person is thinking of absolutely nothing, and stayed there for about a half-hour.

I would one day realize that no female will ever understand this state of mind. I only mention this because it was Mary Fran's bike tire snapping a twig that jerked me out of this zen-like state.

"Whatcha doing, Josh?"

"Just sitting here."

She walked over to my rock and sat down too darn close to me. "Whatcha thinking about?"

"Nothing."

"Oh come on," she elbowed my arm, "how can you not be thinking about anything?"

As I look back on it now, if the kisses hadn't been clue enough, this exchange should have been a dead giveaway. She wanted to know what I was thinking. Yep, she had a crush on me. But what does an eleven-year-old boy know about girls? For that matter, what does a thirty-year-old man, or a fifty-year-old man know about women?

"Did I say I was thinking?"

She looked at me as if a third eye had just opened up in the middle of my forehead. "Well how can you just be sitting there, *not* thinking?"

"Oh never mind, Mary Fran," I said, standing and gathering up my fishing equipment. "How come you came from the direction of my house?"

"I rode my bike out to bring some eggs to Mrs. Jenkins. I stopped at your house on the way back and your mom said you were out here."

"You stopped at my house this early?"

"I didn't knock or anything. I figured if you were up, you'd be outside, doing chores or playing in the barn. I went over to the barn, and I guess your mom must have seen me out the window.

She came out to say hello, and that's when she told me you were down here." I nodded, and Mary Fran continued. "Are we still going to the library today?"

"Sure. We gotta tell Amy about this water. I just wish nine-thirty would come already."

Mary Fran eyed the fishing pole leaning against the tree. "Fishing seems like a great way to pass the time."

"Not anymore. Now, whenever I'm here, all I can think of is all the money I'm not gonna get because *my* treasure is a stream and not a bunch of gold."

Admittedly, I hadn't thought this through. I had not yet figured out how a stream running with healing water could make me rich. Furthermore, whenever I thought about it, I felt a stab of guilt over my greed. It seemed like I shouldn't feel cheated for having this water that could help people, instead of having money.

"Are you kidding?" Mary Fran asked with wide eyes. Her jaw hung agape while she waited for an answer that I didn't have.

"What?"

"It's a *real* elixir!"

"Elixir? What's that?"

"An elixir is a miracle cure-all potion. Back in cowboy times, people got rich selling fake miracle elixirs that *didn't* work. We have a miracle elixir that actually *works*!"

"So we get rich selling stream water?"

"I don't see any reason why not? But first, we have to know everything that it works on, and how *well* it works."

CHAPTER TWENTY-THREE

Memories
(Told by Aggie)

Josh and Mary Fran sat by the stream talking for almost forty-five minutes before they finally decided to go back to his house and ask his mom to make them some breakfast. I thought they'd never leave. I wanted to be sure they were gone before I showed myself, but I was also worried about the other two boys showing up, the tiny boy and the tall, skinny, mischievous looking one. The kids all seemed nice, but I couldn't take a chance on there being any kind of problem with me being on the property. I waited about five minutes after Josh and Mary Fran were out of sight before I came out from the trees and slipped into those blessed waters.

It actually only takes a couple of minutes in the water to feel the effects, but I've always liked to stay in the Brook as long as possible. It's not just the things that the water does for your body. Being in that stream also *feels* remarkably good. When the waters of Grout Brook are doing their thing on you, it feels like you're in a perfectly warmed spa that makes you tingle like a million tiny fingers are massaging you all over.

Although we live in a climate where there aren't many hard

freezes, they *do* occur. I have seen local lakes freeze completely over and I have seen local streams come close. But Grout Brook *never* freezes, and never has even a trace of ice on it. I'd never given this much thought, but it has *never* frozen for as long as I can remember. That's one hundred and forty years. That's right, I'm one hundred and forty years old. I know, I know, that's a long life, but my point is, in all that time, I have *never* seen Grout Brook freeze over.

Anyway, back to Josh and his three friends. I was just getting exceptionally comfortable when I heard a bike rattling up the path, traveling from Nichols Corners Rd. towards Josh's house, and me. I sank deeper into the stream with my head hidden behind a stream-side boulder and stayed as still as I could. As the sound drew closer, I realized it was two bikes. One was just much noisier than the other. At that point, the small boy was still relatively new to the group and I didn't know his name yet. I'd overheard the tall boy's name at a distance and knew that he was Levi or Eli or something like that. The two boys were so busy watching the path and talking to one another that they didn't notice me.

"Why are we going to the library again?" the taller boy asked.

The answer made my stomach churn. "Mary Fran and Josh think we should tell Amy what we found out about the water."

"Oh cripes!" I muttered to myself, worried their loose lips would bring the whole world to the brook.

Each boy cast a nervous glance at the water and for an instant, I thought they'd heard me. But they turned their eyes back to the path in front of them and kept pedaling.

"How come?"

I never heard the answer to that question. They were beyond me by then, and the only thing I heard was the rattling of the bikes. Within minutes, they were out of my sight, and shortly afterward, even the rattling of the bicycles was out of earshot.

Now I could try to forget what I'd just heard, relax, and reacquaint myself with the healing waters of Grout Brook ... and with my memories. That's something you don't think about when you consider the prospect of eternal life, the memories. There are so many of them. For me, they were becoming too numerous to keep straight in my mind. When I was ninety-one, I decided it was time to start writing them down. What I ended up with, was a family history suitable for publication, or so I was told on more than one occasion. The problem was with my identification. You need identification and social security information when you get a book published. I could give them my actual Social Security number, but in this case, the truth would *not* set me free. In fact, it would do the exact opposite. Though I was ninety-one at the time, I looked like I was in my late thirties, and questions about my age would have brought unwanted attention.

But now I've let my mind wander. We can get back to all that later. The point is the memories, the sheer number of them can be overwhelming. You lose people in the depths of your mind, people who were *important* to you. I have found that when I'm relaxing in Grout Brook, I can better recall things. The waters make me feel physically rejuvenated, but they revitalize my mind as well. Sometimes I just go there to sink into the water and let my memories come back into focus. I often get mad because I don't have good mental images of my parents. At those times I come to Grout Brook to sit in the water and remember them.

I get sad when I remember my parents, especially my mother. Grout Brook could have saved her. Sometimes I think I didn't try hard enough to get her out here. But it was a different time. Listening to your elders was still something that young people did, even into their thirties and forties. You just didn't try to convince your parents that you were right and they were wrong. Besides, the idea that the waters gurgling through some stream could cure anything that ailed you was a crazy idea. It still is. If I'd only known that just drinking the water had the same effect, I could have saved her from the cancer that took her at the age of forty-two. Mom refused to see a doctor, and I didn't know cancer by its name back then, but looking back on it now, there's no question about it, it was cancer that killed her. It was different with my father. As it turned out, a fall from a horse took him. He hit his head on a rock and died almost immediately. Grout Brook couldn't have saved him.

I also thought about Millicent, my best friend going all the way back to elementary school. Those days were so very long ago and I miss her so much. There were other friends over the years too, but they just seem to fade into the blackness of all of the passing days. Over time, after the loss of too many friends, you tend to avoid people more and more. The fewer people you know, the fewer people you lose, and the less pain you have to endure. That's another thing about an unusually long life, it tends to turn one into a hermit.

Oh dear! I'd better stop talking about all of this before I get weepy-eyed.

CHAPTER TWENTY-FOUR

Breakfast at the Corey's
(Told by Josh)

Mom was putting the frying pan away while Mary Fran and I started to eat our breakfast. That was when Penny, her tail wagging, jumped to her feet and ran across the kitchen to the side door. After a brief delay, there was a knock. Mom looked outside and saw two more bikes. She rolled her eyes and sighed, but she did it with a smile. She put the pan back on the burner, took last night's leftover potatoes back out, opened the door, and greeted her newest guests in the order that they entered.

"Good morning Mickey, good morning Eli, welcome to Mom's Country Diner. Take your shoes off at the door and have a seat."

Mary Fran and I made eye contact and giggled at Mom.

"Good morning, Mrs. Corey," said Mickey and Eli, as they took off their shoes while fending off Penny's leaping face licks.

"I'm making sausage, eggs, and home fries. What kind of eggs do you boys want?"

"I like scrambled eggs, Mrs. Corey," Eli said quickly.

"Scrambled eggs are fine with me too, ma'am, and thank you, ma'am."

Mom's smile broadened, "You're such a polite boy, Mickey. Your mom taught you well."

Eli's face dropped like Mom had called him a thoughtless boob. Mary Fran and I made smirking eye contact again.

Mickey's face was a little red. "Thank you, Mrs. Corey."

"So what mischief do you kids have planned for today."

"We're going to the library," Mickey said, likely emboldened by my mother's compliment.

I shot him a 'shut-your-pie-hole-before-you-spill-too-many-of-the-beans' glare.

"Oh yeah? The library again? What's with you kids, and what have you done with my real son?"

Now it was my turn to roll my eyes. "Ha ha, very funny Mom. I just like learning stuff, how hard is that to believe?"

She *laughed* at me. I was flabbergasted. My mother actually laughed at the idea that I might want to learn. What kind of a buffoon did she think I was? I narrowed my eyes and gave Mom my most indignant look.

When Mom put on her most pleasant fake smile, I braced myself for the sarcasm I knew was coming. "Well, based on how much trouble I have getting you to sit down and do your homework at night," she said, now nodding at the dog, "I'd say it might be easier to believe that Penny here, is going to fold the laundry for me today."

Not funny. I don't care *how* hard or *how* long Eli, Mary Fran, and Mickey laughed. Traitors!

Though Mom kept her head down while she shoveled breakfast from the skillet onto Eli's and Mickey's plates, I'm pretty sure I saw her lip twitch.

"Maybe I just like learning stuff," I muttered. It did not go unnoticed that Mom and Mary Fran shared a glance and exchanged smirks. I scowled at Mary Fran, gave the other guys a 'keep your traps shut,' look, and continued. "You know we've been trying to learn as much as we can about our farm so we can find the treasure."

Mickey started to open his mouth just then, but Eli put a sharp, fast elbow into his ribs and he got the hint.

After breakfast, we went down to the basement to have

another look at Mr. Hanley's belongings, but almost immediately Mary Fran took note of the big bottles of water in the corner of the basement.

"What do you think those are for?"

"I always figured they were here because nobody wanted to drink the well water, but I'm not so sure anymore. I was wondering if maybe Mr. Hanley filled them up at ..." I never finished the sentence. I didn't have to.

"Well, they didn't come from the water company that way," Mickey said. "I've been to my dad's office and the tops on the jugs they deliver aren't the same. They have blue plastic caps, these are white."

"Maybe he brought water in for the winter."

"To drink or to wash in?"

Eli's question was a good one. I had wondered about Mrs. Devitt. I thought that Mr. Hanley bringing her Jell-O was strange. My mom never gave me Jell-O when I was sick.

"Do you think it works the same way when you drink it?" I asked as I thumbed through some of Mr. Hanley's pictures. The question was posed to all three of my friends, but I didn't expect anyone but Mary Fran to give a coherent answer. She didn't disappoint me.

"I said it before, and I'll say it again. There's only one way to find out. We have to test the idea."

"You want us to *drink* the water from Grout Brook?" Mickey asked.

Based on the look we all gave Mickey, I'm pretty sure we were thinking the same thing. It was Eli who finally put the thought into words.

"Mickey, you swam in that water! Do you know how many mouthfuls you've already gulped down?"

Mickey thought about it for a moment, then nodded. "Okay, but who do we know to test it on? I don't know anybody who's sick. Do you?"

Everyone shook their heads no.

"We should have thought of this sooner," Eli said, "my mom has allergies. She's been clogged up and sneezing all summer, headaches too. She calls them cyanide headaches or something like that."

Mary Fran's look silently posed the question. *Is Eli kidding?*

She smiled to herself and shook her head. "It's sinus headaches, you dope."

Eli hung his head, but his feelings weren't wounded. In fact, he still had that goofy grin on his face. He knew he was supposed to show some sort of contrition when he said something silly. I however, was silently pretty proud of myself. I *knew* that one.

The truth was, I wasn't any smarter than Eli. He was just too nice to pick on me when I displayed my stunning lack of mental horsepower. But *this* time, I got one right.

CHAPTER TWENTY-FIVE

Max
(Told by Josh)

When we got to the library, it was busier than we'd ever seen it before. There were five or six people in line waiting for Amy's help and we knew we'd have to wait a bit. Eli and I went to our regular table and sat down while Mary Fran and Mickey went wandering through the aisles. When Amy saw me and Eli at our table, she smiled and waved at us, but she looked different. She looked like something was bothering her. She had the same smile she always reserved for us, but there was something strange in her eyes as she hurried into the back office and came out with some books for one lady. I convinced myself that it was nothing, that she was just busy.

My attention was diverted from Amy when Mickey came back to the table. He had a book about baseball. When Mary Fran came back, she had a book on the history of the town.

It took about fifteen minutes for Amy to take care of everyone who needed help, and she finally came over to our table and dropped into a chair. We all just stared at her. It was pretty obvious that most of the other kids saw the same thing I saw. She'd always been a bubbly font of enthusiasm, but for the first time we saw her tired … or frustrated … or … something, something not Amy. Nonetheless, she tried to crawl back into her regular, cheerful self.

"Hi kids," she said through a sigh, "how is everyone today?"

"We're great," Eli said. "We think we might have found the treasure. It's not a bunch of money or anything like that, but we figure it's worth *something*."

Though Eli seemed to be oblivious to the *degree* of Amy's distress, the rest of us weren't quite so lacking in observational skills.

"Amy, are you okay?" Mary Fran asked.

"Yeah," I added, "what's the matter? You seem like you don't feel so good."

"I'm sorry, kids. It's just been really busy today. Besides that, my dog, Max, is sick. He's not eating, he vomited some blood, and all he does is lie on his blanket. I took him to the vet this morning before work. And I'm really worried about him." Her voice trembled as she tried to put her smile back on. "But never mind about me. Eli says you think you found the treasure?"

"Well," I explained, "we found something interesting on my family's property, but we aren't sure if it's the *treasure*. That's why we wanted to stop in and see you today. We figured if anyone had any answers, it would be you."

"I'm all ears. But Mary Fran, will you help me get us all some sodas first? Then you guys can tell me all about it."

When Amy and Mary Fran got back with the sodas, I was still gathering my thoughts. I took a long swig of root beer, and then I started. "It may be nothing, but we were all swimming in the creek that runs through our property and something weird happened."

"It sure was weird." Mary Fran said, taking over the storytelling duties. "See, we got in this fight on the bus and met Mickey."

"A fight?"

"Yeah. Derrick Kearny was picking on me and Mary Fran tackled him. Then Eli and Josh jumped on all of us," Mickey explained. "That's how I met these guys."

"Why Mary Fran," Amy couldn't help but grin, "I would never have guessed you were a brawler."

Mary Fran hung her head, more to hide her smile than out of any kind of shame. "It wasn't much of a brawl. I just tackled Derrick. He had it coming. He's a big, fat bully."

"Is that Max?" Mickey asked, pointing to a photo over on Amy's desk. It was a photo of a tan pit bull with a splotch of white fur on its chest.

I glared at Mickey. Amy tumbled back into the dark cloud she'd been in a few minutes ago. Her eyes glistened with tears that I thought would escape at any moment. That was when everything came together in my mind. The old photos of a dog that looked just like Penny, Penny's run from the house every morning, Amy's sick dog ... it hit me like a bolt.

"Yes," she said. "That's my Max."

Max is the one, I thought.

If the waters of Grout Brook were healing waters, who better to heal than Amy's beloved dog. Dogs always drink stream water anyway, and I *already* had my suspicions that Grout Brook was doing some sort of magic on Penny. The idea that Amy might be eternally grateful was not lost on me either. My eyes met Mary Fran's, and I was pretty certain she was thinking the same thing. I was *sure* of it when she spoke. "Aw, poor Max. Do you live in town? Would it be okay if we came to meet Max sometime?"

That was when the tear finally escaped, but Amy wiped it away quickly.

"That's so sweet of you, Mary Fran." Amy jotted down her address on a scrap of paper and handed it to her. "I think Max would *love* to meet you kids. Here's my address, but you probably don't need it. I live right over Clark's General store, just go up the right-hand staircase."

CHAPTER TWENTY-SIX

Hope Springs Eternal
(Told by Amy)

That Saturday, I was at work. I mean I was there physically, but *only* physically. Every part of my heart, my mind, and my soul was across town, at the veterinarian's office where Max was waiting for me. My best friend, my beautiful, fearsome-looking, cuddly dog was dying. It wasn't official, but he'd vomited blood, quit eating, and become lethargic, so we went to the vet. The vet took blood, urine, and stool samples, told me not to stress, and that she'd call me with his test results as soon as she had them. But I didn't need the test results. I had seen all of this before. When I was eight, all of this happened when our German Shepard, Major, died of cancer. I knew I would be alone in months, maybe weeks.

I was grateful that the library was uncharacteristically busy that morning, because for those brief interludes when I was swamped, I was momentarily rescued from the aching of my heart. I'm not talking about some metaphorical aching. I'm talking about a real, *pounding,* physical ache. When I looked up and saw the kids come in, I only got a quick glance at them. There was already a line of people waiting to ask questions, pay fines, or check out books, and I was busy getting them all taken care of. When I looked up again, Josh and Eli were at our regular work table. I gave them a smile and a little wave. No matter how much I was hurting, it wasn't their fault, and I was determined to be my normal cheerful self … or at least to try. As it turned out, this was more easily said than done.

Eventually, I checked out *A Sanctuary Built of Words* and *Looking for Wild Things* for Mrs. Byron, and I collected a dollar and forty cents in fines from Mrs. Carey for her tardy return of *Say Cheese and Murder*. That was the end of my line of customers and within a few minutes, the library fell still again. I went into the little break room behind the front desk to get sodas for the kids, but I was overwhelmed with thoughts of Max and forgot why I'd gone in there. I washed my face, drank the last of my iced tea, put on my best happy face, and went out to meet with my band of young treasure-hunters.

"Hi kids, how is everyone today?" I asked as I sat down with them at our regular table.

Eli was excited and immediately started to tell me about something they found that he thought was the treasure. Mary Fran, however, zeroed in on me and knew immediately that something was wrong. Josh followed her lead, and they pressed me on it. I told them that Max was ill, no details, and tried to turn the topic back away from me, but their questions had re-started the dull throb in my chest. The tears rose behind whatever dam usually holds them back, and I was back in my dark vortex. The word 'Max' flashed in my mind with every pulse of hurt that passed through my heart. I bounced back and forth between hope that I knew was false, and the reality that my dog was going to die. I needed to escape. I didn't want the kids to see me break down so I tried to change the subject. "But never mind about me. Eli said you think you found the treasure?"

Josh started to explain that they'd found something that they thought *could* be the treasure, but my mind was still on Max, and I still felt like I might lose it. I remembered that I'd never gotten the sodas and I jumped from the table. "I'm all ears, but Mary Fran, will you help me get us all some sodas first? Then you guys can tell me all about it."

101

I thought my tears and I had escaped, but as I had asked, Mary Fran followed to help with the sodas.

"Miss Amy, are you sure you're okay?"

"Sure Mary Fran. I'll be fine. I'm just a little tired." She bought my excuse and we brought the sodas out.

I'm not sure if what the kids were telling me just didn't sink in, or if I didn't believe what they were saying, but when they first began to explain what they believed to be true about Grout Brook, I didn't make the connection. Perhaps it was just the fog of grief enshrouding me. Whatever it was, I didn't immediately connect the plight of my dog with what these kids were telling me, but slowly, gradually it began to sink in.

At first, I was devoting all of my energy to trying to keep thoughts about Max out of my mind and off my facial expressions. I listened intently, but with all of the normal skepticism of any adult listening to a fanciful children's tale. I was amused and more than a little bit impressed by the story of Mary Fran taking down the bigger bully. I was feeling a little better. In fact, I almost let out a laugh. But then little Mickey pointed to my desk and asked if that was a picture of Max and I started to come apart again.

Mary Fran asked if they could come and meet Max sometime soon.

It will have to be really soon, was what I thought, but I kept my happy face.

"That's so sweet of you, Mary Fran. I think Max would *love* to meet you kids. Here's my address, but you probably don't need it I live right over Clark's General store, you go up the right hand staircase."

"Sure," Mary Fran said, "everybody knows where that is."

That was when Josh blurted out the words that would change my life. "Amy, the water in Grout Brook is magic. It can help Max."

"What?" I heard what he said, I just needed him to repeat it. In my mind, I knew it was just a child's flight of fancy, but my heart demanded that I hear the words again.

Breathless, he went on, talking faster with each word. "When we first moved in, I cut myself while I was fishing, and when I waded in Grout Brook, my cut *healed*."

102

"Then I cut my knee in that fight with Derrick Kearny," Mary Fran added, "and we all went swimming in Josh's stream that day, and *my* cut healed."

Eli jumped in next. "Yeah, and it fixed my face after I fell. It was like it never even *happened*."

I couldn't help but let out a little gasp.

"Can we bring Max some water?" Josh asked, "Please?"

I thought about what *I* had discovered about the property. If those waters really were healing waters, that might explain how Caleb Hanley *could* have lived all those years. It was insane, but maybe he *was* born 145 years ago. Maybe he *could* have lived forever if he hadn't been shot. I knew it was madness, but it fed my hope, and I *wanted* to find reasons to believe this fantastical claim. I decided that I could believe in magic for the sake of these kids. *Hey*! We do it with Santa Claus, don't we?

I gathered myself and spoke. "When would you like to come and meet him?"

CHAPTER TWENTY-SEVEN

Prescription For Life
(Told by Amy)

I checked my messages after I closed up the library and there was a single message ... from the vet's office. They had test results. Even before I knew what the results *were*, my heart slammed into my throat. The hope that it might end up being nothing was dissipating like the morning fog. If my gut feeling that I was about to get bad news wasn't enough, there was the obvious sadness in the voice of the receptionist who left the message. As I drove to the vet's office to get the news that I knew was going to break my heart, I kept wiping away what felt like one persistent tear, determined to get to the bottom of my face, and my heart. She asked me to come into the office area, away from other customers.

The lump in my throat thickened when she motioned toward the chair and asked me to have a seat. She showed me a picture of an X-ray and went into an explanation of what I was looking at. Nothing between the words 'cancer', and 'consider his pain' registered. I was stunned. I shouldn't have been. That feeling in the pit of my stomach had been whispering the word ever since I'd noticed that something was wrong with Max. I was anxious to get home and love my dog. The time I had left to love my Maxy was short.

On the way home, while Max slept next to me, the thought of Grout Brook's supposedly healing waters passed through my mind, but I dismissed those thoughts as wishful thinking. Now was a time for reality, awful reality. What I finally did while driving home, was break down into tears. Once at home, I sat in my car, looking away from Max until I stopped crying. As silly as it might seem, I didn't want him to see me crying.

I carried Max upstairs, and inside. I didn't ask him to come up on the sofa or the bed. I didn't want him to spend an extra ounce of energy doing that. Instead, I laid down next to him on the floor, put my arm around him, and silently cried myself to sleep.

I was disoriented when I woke up. Normally, when you wake up, it's morning and you're in your bed. But I was on the floor … and the sun was pouring in through the window. It wasn't morning, it couldn't be. Mine was one of two apartments above Clark's General Store. As it was on the west side of the building, I never got morning sun. Eventually, I remembered the whole, terrible day, and realized that I'd simply fallen asleep on the living room floor. Though still slightly disoriented, I was comforted by the smell of Max, and the softness of his fur against my face.

Then the knocking came again.

That's what woke me up! I thought. *Who's knocking at my door? The only people I know are people from work.*

I grabbed the sofa, pulled myself to my feet, and tried to straighten my hair and clear my mind as I walked to the door. I nudged the curtains aside to look out the window on my door. I couldn't help but smile. I needed that smile. I wiped my still red eyes and pulled the door open.

"Josh, Mary Fran! What are you doing here?"

"You told us we could come over and meet Max," Josh said, clearly a little confused at my question.

"Yeah," Mary Fran added, "you even told us where you lived."

Of course, I knew that, but I was groggy, and I guess I didn't expect them to take me up on it … at least not so soon.

"Well come in, come in," I pulled the door farther open and

stepped back. "Don't just stand out there on the porch. Come on in."

Mary Fran was in front and entered first. It wasn't until Josh came in that I noticed the two-liter soda bottle in his hand. The label said Pepsi, but it was obvious there was a clear liquid inside; water, I assumed.

"We can't stay long. Me and Josh rode into town with my mom. She's downstairs in the store getting a few things."

"You should have brought her up with you," I said, still trying to straighten my hair and clear my mind. "I'd like to meet her."

Max was up now and greeting the kids with what enthusiasm he could muster. His tail wagged weakly as he stood by my side and licked Mary Fran's hand slowly. Josh kneeled next to Mary Fran, gently petting Max's head.

"Uhm, she doesn't really know we're up here."

"Yeah," Josh added, petting Max with both hands. He nodded towards the bottle he'd set on the floor. "We have to go soon. We just wanted to bring you this water for Max."

"You make sure to give Max that water," Mary Fran wagged her finger at me. "It will help."

I wanted so badly to believe her, but my heart was losing the battle with my mind. My poor Max seemed to be getting weaker by the minute.

Mary Fran joined Josh in a kneeling position to give Max a few more loving strokes before she jumped back to her feet.

"Come on, Josh, we better go before my mom gets back to the car."

My sadness returned as I stood on my porch, waving goodbye to the children. They were just the sweetest kids.

"You make sure you put that water in Max's bowl!" Josh called as he disappeared into the back seat.

I went inside, looked at the bottle of water by the door, and sat on the floor with my back against the sofa. Max came over, laid down next to me, rested his head on my lap and I scratched his head. Ninety minutes later, when we got up to go to bed, I glanced over at the bottle and started down the hallway, but something made me stop. I went back out front, got the bottle, emptied Max's water bowl, and filled it with the water that Josh and Mary Fran had brought. At the very least, I'd be able to let the kids know that I believed in them. I might have been losing Max, but I didn't have to lose those kids.

CHAPTER TWENTY-EIGHT

Missed The Bus
(Told by Josh)

It had been almost two weeks since Dad said I should tell Eli about the Mary Fran situation. It wasn't like I was ignoring Dad's advice. I was just waiting for the right time. Every time I started to do it, I got that same feeling in the pit of my stomach that I got when I had to tell Mom I got in trouble at school.

Mary Fran kissing me was like when I ate the candy Mom kept in her secret hiding spot. I liked it plenty, but deep down inside, I felt like I shouldn't be doing it. It's weird how you get the same feeling in your stomach when you're dreading something, that you get when you're really hoping for something to happen. I guess I could have been avoiding Eli and Mary Fran in the hopes that the problem would work itself out. But Monday when Mary Fran saw me in the hall at school, things got dicey again.

"Hey Josh," she said as she ran to catch up with me, "where have you been? Have you been avoiding me?"

"Uh, hey Mary Fran ... no, uh ... I haven't been ... I mean ..." She didn't let me finish.

"What's the matter? Did I do something to make you – ?"

"*No*," I protested before she could finish her question. "It's just that ..." At that point, I realized that, with my last three words, I'd all but admitted that something *was* wrong. I also realized that three of Mary Fran's friends were watching us. That was when I felt the redness crawling up my face. "Look, I'm gonna be late for science class, can we talk about this at Big Oak after school?"

The worry was etched on her face almost as clearly as the disappointment on the faces of her three friends when they realized they weren't going to have ringside seats to our interpersonal drama.

"Okay, Josh," she kicked at a gum wrapper her toe, "just as long as I didn't do anything to hurt your feelings."

"No, no, no, Mary Fran," I said, shaking my head, waving my palms at her, and backing away as fast as I could. "It's nothing like that. It's no big deal, really."

I had a brief moment of relief as I disappeared into the crowd of kids, but that moment vaporized when I almost walked right into Eli.

"Hey, Josh. Was that Mary Fran you were talking to?"

"Huh?"

"What were you guys talking about? Did she say anything about me? I haven't seen her in a while. If I didn't know better, I'd swear she was avoiding me."

"No Eli," I said, searching for the right answer. I wondered how long he'd been watching, and if he'd noticed the pained look on her face. "It was nothing. We were just passing in the hall and said hello."

"Oh, okay. Well, I better scram. I want to try to catch her. I'm going to ask her to next Friday's dance."

"Oh ... uhm," I gulped, "good luck."

He smiled a big, hopeful smile and took off down the hall in the same general direction that Mary Fran had gone. My stomach churned, as it would for the remainder of the school day. I hoped he wouldn't catch up with her.

I missed the bus and had to call Mom to come and get me for the seventh time in the last ten school days. To my amazement, she was on to me. She started grilling me as soon as I got in the car.

"Are you trying to avoid your friends because of the Eli

and Mary Fran situation?"

I was stunned. *How the ...*

"Your father told me all about it." She explained, not making me ask the question. "You haven't told Eli yet, have you?"

Apparently, at that age, I thought my mom was about as sharp as a bowling ball, *and* it hadn't occurred to me that she and Dad ever had meaningful conversations.

"It's not that I'm ignoring what Dad told me," I said. "It's just that I haven't really figured out how to tell Eli yet. And *now*, I went and made it worse because Mary Fran figured out that I've been avoiding her and *she* thinks I'm mad at her. She darn near cried in school."

"So what are you going to do?"

"Gonna meet her out at Big Oak when we get home and tell her what's going on. I have to tell her why I been avoiding her. I gotta tell her that Eli wants to ask her to next weekend's dance too, if he didn't already ask her."

"There's a dance coming up?"

"Yeah."

"Why didn't you tell me? Are you going? Who are you going to ask?"

"No," I said, then tossed out another lie. "I'm not into dances all that much."

"I thought you told your father that you sort of liked it when Mary Fran kissed you."

Mercifully, we were home now. "Gotta go," I yelled over my shoulder as I jumped out of the car. "Mary Fran's waiting."

Once again, it felt good to escape an uncomfortable situation, but once again, I was being short-sighted. I was on my bike and halfway to Big Oak when it sank in that I was hurrying away from Mom to get to my rendezvous with Mary Fran.

Yikes!

I was out of the frying pan and pedaling as hard as I could to get to the fire, and I hadn't a clue how I was going to tell Mary Fran what I was feeling. For that matter, I didn't have any idea how, exactly, it was that I felt.

CHAPTER TWENTY-NINE

The Impossible Boy
(Told by Josh)

By the time I was a hundred feet from Big Oak I was riding as slowly as a person could go on a bike without tipping over. Another fifty feet and I'd pedal around the bend in the path. Then, there would be no turning back. Maybe I'd catch a break. Maybe Mary Fran wouldn't be there. I got off my bike and walked it around the bend in the trail, preserving my 'emergency eject" option for a few more precious seconds. Miraculously, when I turned the corner, she *wasn't* there. Saved! I was there at the agreed upon time and *she* wasn't.

I'm off the hoo-

"Hey, Josh." Reflexively, I tilted my head back, closed my eyes, and let out a groan.

"Hey, Mary Fran."

"What's the matter? Why did you groan like that?" *Cripes!* I thought, *she can see I'm disgusted.* "Don't you want to talk to me?"

When I opened my eyes, I saw Mary Fran as I'd never seen her before. Her eyes were red and had the glisten of tears. When she hung her head, I felt a twinge of pain in my chest. All these years later, I'm certain that pain was guilt. I put on the worst fake smile ever, and tried to smooth things over.

"No! I mean … no, that's not it. Why wouldn't I want to talk to you? We're friends."

"I *thought* we were," she said.

Ouch!

"What's *that* supposed to mean Mary Fran? Of *course* we're friends."

"Then why have you been avoiding me? I thought you liked it when we kissed."

"What do you mean when *we* kissed? *We* didn't kiss. *You* kissed *me* … look … Mary Fran … it's more complicated than that."

"How?"

"I liked it alright when you … I mean … I didn't … I mean … I don't hate when you … you know. It's just that, a little while ago … Eli told me … well, he said ..."

"Eli told you he liked me?"

I let out a sigh. *Oh, thank you, Mary Fran. I swear I could kiss y … No, wait … no kissing … no more kissing!*

"Yeah, and Eli's my best friend. I don't want to hurt my best friend like that."

"He asked me to the dance today."

My heart jumped into my throat and sat up there, worrying about Eli. "What did you say?"

"I told him maybe."

I exhaled. 'Maybe' was better than 'no'.

"Why not yes?"

"Isn't that obvious? I was waiting … hoping *you'd* ask me to the dance."

"Well, *I* can't ask you."

"Why not? I know girls who would be nice for Eli."

Yeah, I thought, *like one of your three goofball friends who were in the hall with you today?*

I opened my mouth, thinking I was going to answer her, but I realized I didn't have an answer … at least not one I could give her. My mouth hung open. I was dumbfounded. 'What are you, stupid?' didn't seem like the right reply. It seemed mean. I didn't want her to start bawling again. I had already tried to tell her that I didn't want to hurt Eli. She didn't seem to comprehend that. I was at a complete loss. How could she always be so much smarter than us, and at the same time be so dense?

"Hey, guys." A third voice turned our heads and our attention up the trail.

"Mickey!" I almost squealed.

Mary Fran shot me a look. Apparently, I'd greeted Mickey a bit too enthusiastically. But I couldn't help it. I had never been happier to see him.

Mickey Brown for the block.

"Hi, Mickey," Mary Fran said with all of the enthusiasm one normally reserves for a dental visit.

"Hi, Mary Fran, hey, Josh, your mom said to send you home. She wants you to ride your bike into town for her."

Mickey Brown for the win! We'd just come back from town. So somehow, Mom must have known I might need bailing out.

I jumped on my bike, determined to get out of there before fate decided to cut off my escape route, but I couldn't resist turning back to Mary Fran.

"I can't do that thing we were talking about. But you talk to Eli. I'm sure he'd be happy to do it for you."

Hands on hips, she stomped. "Josh Corey, you're impossible!"

I may be impossible, I thought as I pedaled back toward home as fast as I could, *but I didn't let you make me hurt my best friend, and you're not crying anymore.*

CHAPTER THIRTY

The Pasta Errand
(Told by Josh)

You don't realize how many different kinds of pasta there are until you're standing in the aisle at the store, trying to remember what kind your mom usually buys. It turned out, Mom had just forgotten to stop at the store on the way home. She'd sent me into town on my bike to get a box of pasta, and I had absolutely *no* idea what brand or shape of pasta to get. To make matters worse, I'd gone to the candy counter first to put a Hershey Bar in my shopping basket, so I was also mentally subtracting the price of the candy bar from the money Mom had given me.

When the arm came around my neck from behind, several thoughts passed through my mind. In that fraction of a second, my first thought was that it was Derrick Kearny, and he was there for vengeance, to settle the score from the school bus fiasco.

No, this person smells good. That eliminates Derrick Kearny.
I've smelled this nice smell before.
Is that hair tickling my head and the back of my neck?
I know that smell. That's ... Amy!

"Josh Corey, I could just kiss you!" The voice that derailed my half-second train of thought confirmed my conclusion. It *was* Amy.

Did she say ... she could kiss me? I asked myself. I was a half-second behind what was happening and futilely trying to calm my heartbeat. *By all means, if you feel that you must.*

She spun me around to face her and held me by my shoulders. Her face displayed a mix of signs that perplexed me at first. The tears didn't match her enormous smile. My mind flashed back to the time we lived in our old house, and a neighbor called to tell Mom that he'd passed an accident scene on the road. He saw Dad's car, and it was badly torn up. While he was telling Mom all about it, there was a knock on the front door. When Mom and I looked out the window and saw a police car, she hung up on the neighbor and was in tears before she reached the door. When she opened it and Dad was there, standing next to the police officer, her face did this same thing – tears, and a smile. I understood it now, but I still wasn't clear on why it was there. Apparently, my confusion showed.

"Max," she said, "Max is alright now. The tumors are gone! His X-rays are clean!"

It had been more than a week since Mary Fran and I brought that Grout Brook water to Amy for her to give to Max. To be honest, I never realized Max was *that* sick when we gave Amy the water. We had no doubt that Max would feel better. Secure in the belief that Max was going to be fine, I'd forgotten all about it.

"Tumors?"

"He had cancer, Josh. He had cancer and it's *gone* now! He saw the vet today and his X-rays are clean. The vet can't explain it, but I can. He's all better!"

She pulled me to her and clutched me in a hug the likes of which I had *never* experienced before. I wasn't old enough to completely understand why, but that hug fogged up my brain. In an effort to keep my wits about me, I tried to focus on my mission.

Why am I here again?

You came here for Mom, you moron!

I did? What am I supposed to get, this candy bar? She's still hugging me. I like this.

Pasta, you idiot, you're supposed to get pasta! Now snap

out of it.

Mercifully, or not, Amy let go of me and the tide of reality washed back over me. I had my wits about me again - well, mostly. The smell of Amy's perfume would both torment and delight me for the rest of the day, but the gravity of what she told me was managing to sink in. Had the waters of Grout Brook cured cancer? It seemed that they had. Even as a *kid*, I understood the significance of this. Maybe we *did* have a valuable treasure here.

"You didn't tell the vet about the water we brought you, did you?"

"No Josh. That's *your* secret, and your decision whether to talk about it or not."

"Thanks, my folks think that maybe we should keep it quiet for now."

I was lying. As far as I knew, my parents knew nothing about the healing waters. I hadn't told them yet because I didn't think they'd believe it. I was afraid they'd think I was just being a stupid kid.

"Don't worry Josh, your secret is safe with me, but maybe I could get a bottle of water each week ... for Max?"

"Sure!" I said, not waiting for any further explanation. "No problem."

The feeling that Amy would be counting on me felt almost as good as that hug had felt. It would take some time for me to realize that what I was feeling was a messy mix of power, physical attraction, and mind-numbing happiness.

Eventually, I remembered why I was there, and I grabbed a box of elbow macaroni. After I paid at the register, we went up to her apartment above the store so I could see Max. He was like a different dog. As soon as I came in, he was paws up and on my chest, standing almost as tall as me, and licking me in the face. After I played with him for a few minutes and said I had to leave, Amy insisted on giving me a ride home. We put my bike in the back of Amy's pickup truck, and Max sat between us in the cab.

As we pulled up at the traffic light, Amy broke the silence.

"You know, there was something else I found out about your property when I was doing research for your treasure hunt. It didn't make any sense to me then, but now I'm beginning to understand."

"Really? What is it?"

"According to birth records in the village clerk's office, Caleb Hanley was over 145 years old when he died. At first, I thought it was some sort of a clerical mistake, but it wasn't just his birth records. The property records say that the farm was titled to Caleb Hanley in August of 1855. At first, I thought this Caleb Hanley was his grandfather, but there weren't any more changes of title until the county assumed ownership after Mr. Hanley died. Then it showed your parents buying the place." She paused and looked over at me. "Do you understand what that means?"

I was only eleven, but I wasn't a doofus.

"Well, if it was our Mr. Hanley who bought the house, he'd have to be pretty old." Now it was my turn to pause and look over at *her*. "So you think the stream is some kind of ... fountain of youth too?"

"You know about the fountain of youth?"

"Yeah, we learned about Ponce DeLeon in school. But our teacher told us he searched for the fountain of youth in Florida and never found it. Do you think Grout Brook is the real fountain of youth?"

"I don't know, Josh. All I know is what it did for Max, and ... if I ever ... get really sick ..."

"You don't have to say it ... I'll bring you some water any time you ask me to."

"Or let me go swimming?"

"I'd have to ask my parents. It would be better to ask if you can fish in our stream. I'd ask Mom for you, she's the one I always ask if I really want to get a yes." I pointed to my driveway. "This is where I live. I can get out at the end of the driveway, you don't have to take me all the way down to the house."

Amy smiled and turned into our driveway. "Well, do you need help getting your bike out of the back?"

"Nah, I can get it."

I wanted Amy to see me as strong and grown up. I hopped out of the truck, hitched my jeans up, pulled my bike out of the bed, and started to get on my bike.

"Hey, Josh," Amy yelled.

I stopped and turned around with my chest puffed out as much as a skinny eleven-year-old's chest *can* be puffed out.

"Yeah?" I squeaked in an embarrassingly kid-like voice. In my mind, I cringed.

"You forgot your pasta and candy bar."

Great, just great! Really adult. I sounded like a girl, *and* I forgot my stuff like a dumb kid.

"Oh, uh, thanks Amy." I dropped the bike and ran back to her truck, and she gave me the bag and a smile.

As I rode my bike down the driveway, the smell of Amy's hair wafted up from my shirt, swirled around my head, and kept me drunk with the memory of our new found closeness.

That night I slept with my shirt, between me and my pillow.

CHAPTER THIRTY-ONE

Not Yet!
(Told by Josh)

Things began to normalize over the next week or so. Make no mistake about it, the effects of Amy's kiss would *never* wear off. I just accepted the fact that I loved Amy and one day I'd marry her. This was a revelation that didn't have to be spelled out to Mary Fran. She just needed to know that I wasn't receptive to her kisses anymore. One might think that this would be an easy message to convey for an eleven-year-old boy who'd only recently grown out of his cootiphobia, that's fear of cooties for the medically unsophisticated.

The truth was that I *did* still kind of like it when Mary Fran kissed me, but it had a nagging feeling of wrongness to it. I knew my heart was with Amy and my liking to have Mary Fran kiss me wasn't about liking Mary Fran. I just liked being kissed. But hurting Mary Fran's feelings was not in the same time zone with 'easy'. I found that the best policy was simply to try never to be alone with her. The few times that I did find myself alone with her, I went to plan B.

To this day I don't think she ever figured out that I could let loose with a loud, obnoxious belch on demand. I'm not talking about your run of the mill, garden-variety belch. This belch sounded like a cross between the croak of a six hundred pound bullfrog and the roar of a cranky T-Rex. Who knew a girl would find the prospect of kissing someone who'd just let loose such a masterpiece of a belch to be unappealing?

She never said anything, but after the first few days of this kiss-avoidance campaign, I would occasionally see a trace of hurt in her eyes. It usually happened when Eli would start to go someplace or do something that might leave me alone with Mary Fran, and I'd hurriedly volunteer to go with him.

This was what happened that first Tuesday in October when my mom called Eli into our house. A moment of incidental eye-contact with Mary Fran told me that she was the predator and I was potential prey, so I jumped up to go inside with Eli. Mom had called him in because *his* mom was on the phone and wanted to talk to him. It was a brief, typical 'mom phone call.' Are you behaving? Do you have a lot of homework? When are you coming home? Mary Fran came in just a moment before Eli hung up. His mother wanted him to come home, he had to go ... to finish his homework.

That was when Mom put me in a lurch. "Honey, I have to go over to Mrs. Devitt's house, but there are hot dogs and leftover mashed potatoes in the fridge. You and Mary Fran can warm those up for dinner. Your father will be done in the fields in about an hour."

When I caught Mary Fran's flicker of a smile, I panicked and played the only card I had. I *needed* to go with Mom.

"Why do you have to go to Mrs. Devitt's house?"

When Mom said, "she called and said she doesn't feel well. I want to go and check on her," it felt like all of the air left the room.

My eyes met Mary Fran's and the predator in her eyes was gone. I had no doubt that we were both thinking the same thing. The water! We could help Mrs. Devitt.

"Why are *you* the one who has to go check on her?" I asked.

"She's all alone in the world, sweetie. She doesn't have anyone to look after her."

"Is she bad sick?" Mary Fran asked.

"Can we go with you?" I asked before Mom could answer Mary Fran.

Mom's expression told me she didn't think that was a good idea, and she was trying to find the words to say 'no', without hurting our feelings.

"If she has to go to the hospital, you may need help getting her to your car," Mary Fran added.

Mom's eyebrow twitched upward with the corner of her mouth. She relented. "That might be a good idea."

Mary Fran had turned Mom around 180 degrees in an instant. I was impressed.

Then Mom turned to me. "Josh, you come on upstairs and change out of your school clothes while I take this laundry up to my bedroom. Mary Fran, will you be okay down here by yourself for a few minutes?"

"Yes ma'am," Mary Fran said, shooting me a conspiratorial glance, "is it okay if I get a bottle of water?"

"Sure honey. I think there are still some cold ones in the fridge."

I changed clothes in record time and hurried back downstairs where Mary Fran sat, wiping the outside of a bottle of water with a paper towel.

"Is this the water from – "

"It's the right water," she said before I could finish, "I emptied a bottle from the fridge and filled it downstairs."

Over the previous week, thanks to a few cuts, scratches and bruises, we had verified that the water in the big blue jugs in the basement was *indeed,* water from Grout Brook.

When we got inside Mrs. Devitt's place, we all gasped audibly. Mrs. Devitt, who was lying on her sofa, was a shadow of her normal self. She didn't appear to weigh more than ninety pounds, and she was horribly pale. Now I understood what adults meant when they said someone looked like death warmed over.

"Oh my God!" my mother said, hurrying to the kitchen. "I'll be right back. I'm going to go call Alice Farley. "

Alice was a nurse who lived in town. Neither Mom nor Mrs. Devitt really knew Alice. It was just that in an emergency, most people in town called Alice because she could get to them much faster than the ambulance.

"She looks really bad," Mary Fran whispered to me.

I swallowed hard, and a tear started to slide down my cheek. "I don't know if the water's going to work."

Mary Fran didn't speak, but the look on her face told me that she shared my doubts. Finally, she snapped out of the stupor, and bolted over to Mrs. Devitt. She gently raised the old woman to a sitting position, unscrewed the bottle, and brought it up to her lips.

"Here Mrs. Devitt. This will make you feel better."

At first, Mrs. Devitt choked, and spilled more water than she drank. It seemed almost as if she was fighting the water. As the seconds crawled by and I heard Mom's urgent but muffled voice in the kitchen, where she was talking to Alice on the phone. Gradually, it began to look more like Mrs. Devitt was drinking the water. She blinked her eyes two or three times, took the bottle from Mary Fran, took one more big swallow, sat the water on the end table, and pushed herself up into a more comfortable sitting position.

"Josh, Mary Fran!" she said. "What are you kids doing here? Goodness, I must look a sight."

We went nearly mute with amazement. It was like Mrs. Devitt had risen from the dead right in front of our eyes.

"Uh ... we ... uhm ... came over with my mom." I stammered. "Someone told her that you were –"

My mom was in a near-breathless panic as she came rushing back in. "Okay kids, I called Alice and she should be over in –"

She stopped in her tracks and her jaw fell open at the sight of Mrs. Devitt sitting up. Mom's jaw stayed agape for a few seconds before Mrs. Devitt broke the silence.

"Jennifer, what's the matter? You look like you've seen a ghost. Why did you call Alice? Is someone sick?"

CHAPTER THIRTY-TWO

Absolute Power Disrupts
(Told by Josh)

There was an unsettling quiet in the car on the way back from Mrs. Devitt's house. Mom was visibly out of sorts after what we'd seen. I thought about telling her about Grout Brook, but I held my tongue. Looking back on that night, I'm ashamed to say that, at first, I didn't tell her because I liked the feeling of having knowledge and power. As a kid, you go to your parents to gain knowledge. Growing up, they are our all-knowing beings, and I admit it, I liked knowing something that Mom and Dad did not, and the power! Even at eleven years old, I realized that we now held the tremendous power of life and death. Us ... kids ... we had authority over nature, over the universe ... almost like God.

But when we dropped Mary Fran off, she and I shared a look that said, 'I'm scared.' Then we exchanged weak smiles.

"Uhm ... I'll see you tomorrow, Josh."

"Yeah, see ya."

Mary Fran got out, closed the door, Mom waited to be sure she was safely inside, and we headed for home. When we got there, Mom was *still* bothered. This was probably why she didn't notice that I was troubled too. You would think I would have been happy, even ecstatic about Mrs. Devitt's turnaround. But at some point during the ride home, I wondered how many people who we could have saved, had died that night.

Mom dove right into housework as she always did when something was bugging her. When I saw Dad's newspaper on the end table by his recliner, I took it up to my room and started thumbing through the pages. I knew that somewhere in there was a place where they told you who'd died in the last several days. At eleven years old, I didn't know they called that the obituaries. It was written right there on the page, but at eleven, if you even bothered to look at the paper, you never even slowed down on that page.

Three people were listed as having died recently and although I didn't know them, I felt like I did. Worse than that, I felt like I'd failed them, like they were hanging from a cliff and I was holding their hands. Mine had been the hand that kept them from the pit of death, and I'd allowed them to slip from my grasp.

There was George Matthews, who'd died at home two days earlier after a prolonged illness, Eva Walters, who passed away gently at the Peaceful Gardens Senior Care Home, and Alan Krause, a victim of an automobile accident on the previous night.

At least Mr. Krause's demise allowed me the comfort of knowing that I couldn't have helped him. He was gone in an instant. Mr. Matthews was not so easy on my conscience though … thirteen grandchildren. I remembered how I cried when my grandpa passed away. I wondered how many of those grandchildren were still crying tonight because they'd lost their grandpa, and how many would never even know him. There was little written about Eva Walters, but there *was* a photo of her, taken in her younger days. When you're a kid, old people are just old people. It never occurs to you that they were once handsome young men and beautiful young women. Eva Walters had once looked alarmingly like Amy, my Amy. My stomach churned, my hands began to tremble, and my eyes filled with tears, but I held them back.

Suddenly, I didn't like the feeling of power all that much. At that moment I wanted to tell Mom and Dad about Grout Brook, let them worry about life and death, and wash my hands of the whole thing. But I chose not to, not because I enjoyed having this power to myself, but because *now* I realized what a terrible thing it would be to drop on their shoulders.

How would *you* decide who lives and who dies? What if someone came looking for that life-saving water and you weren't home, perhaps you were off on vacation? Could you ever leave home knowing that your being away could be the difference between someone living or dying? My father had left his corporate lifestyle to escape the stress that his doctor had warned would kill him. How could I put the lives and deaths of people he didn't even know in his lap?

I got up and took a walk downstairs. I could hear Mom doing something in the kitchen as I walked back over by Dad's chair and started to put the paper down, but for some reason I picked it up again.

"Josh, is that you?" came Mom's voice from the kitchen.

I opened the paper to the obituaries again and folded it so I could hold it with one hand. "Yeah, Mom."

"You've been quiet. Are you okay?"

Since we'd left Mrs. Devitt's house, the whole world had been quiet.

"Yeah," I said, looking at the photo of a young Eva Walters, "I was just thinking about Mrs. Devitt."

I was talking to Mom, but Eva Walters was talking to me. She was reminding me that Mrs. Devitt was once a young woman, maybe a beautiful young woman like Amy. Eva was whispering in my ear. *No one escapes the grasp of time, Josh.*

But maybe we could.

That was when Mom came into the living room with a pan in her hand and a dishcloth over her shoulder. As she walked toward me, I casually laid the paper on the table, taking care to put the side with the obituaries face down.

She put the pan down on top of the newspaper and hugged me. "That visit to Mrs. Devitt upset you, didn't it? I shouldn't have brought you kids with me. I'm sorry."

"I'm okay, Mom. Gee, we're not babies. I saw Grandma when she was sick."

Before Mom could say anything, the phone rang and she

picked it up.

"Hello, Corey residence."

"Oh, hi sweetie. Yes, he's right here." She handed me the phone and said, "Honey, it's Mary Fran. I'll go back in the kitchen and let you two talk." I took the phone and sat in Dad's chair. Mom picked up her already dry pan and resumed drying it as she walked back into the kitchen.

There were no pleasantries, no 'hello', no 'hi, Josh', just a question posed in a subdued voice that I'd never before heard come from Mary Fran's mouth.

"You okay?"

She had obviously been just as affected as Mom and I.

"I don't know."

"I'm scared," she said. I tried to answer, but the answer got caught in my throat, so she went on. "Do you think we're grown up enough to be in charge of this?"

"I don't know," I twirled the phone cord around my finger while I contemplated the rest of my answer. "This is pretty important stuff. Should we talk about it?"

"How about tomorrow morning?" she suggested. "Meet me at Big Oak?"

"Come over to my house first, we'll have breakfast. Better stop and get Eli and Mickey too."

"Okay, Mary Fran, see you in the morning."

CHAPTER THIRTY-THREE

The Newsletter
(Told by Josh)

I was on the front porch swing waiting when Mary Fran and Mickey rode up on their bikes Saturday morning. I was too comfortable to get off the swing.

"Hey guys, where's Eli? I thought you were going to get him too."

Mary Fran answered as they got off their bikes and let them fall in the yard next to the sidewalk, where they always did.

"He's coming. He woke up late. The bum was still in his pajamas."

I glanced down at my pajama bottoms, and back up at Mary Fran. We exchanged sheepish smiles. "Did you tell Mickey about Mrs. Devitt?"

"Yeah," Mickey rolled his eyes, "but I wasn't born yesterday. You guys must think I'm a real goober."

Mary Fran held her hands out at her sides, palms up, and let out a sigh. "He thinks we're pulling his leg."

"Mickey, you saw what happened to Mary Fran's knee the other day. No more cut, no scar, no nothing."

"I didn't see her knee up close. Maybe that was somebody

127

else's blood and it just washed off in the water."

"Okay, fine Mickey, I don't expect you to believe us right away. You have to see it first hand. Heck, I thought I believed it, but I didn't *really* believe it until I saw what I saw last night. Did Mary Fran tell you about last night?"

"Yeah, she told me what you guys *say* happened last night."

Mary Fran rolled her eyes. "Mickey," she said, throwing her hands up in disgust, "we saw it with our own eyes."

"Mary Fran, don't worry about it." I turned to Mickey, "You'll see that we're not crazy quick enough. But for now, can you just pretend you believe us?"

That was when Mom interrupted us from the kitchen. "Josh! Are you kids coming in to eat breakfast or not?"

"We're still waiting for Eli, Mom. Mary Fran says he won't be long."

"Okay, honey."

We both looked back at Mickey. "Alright, so let's say you two aren't loony, and you have a stream full of magic water running through your property. What do you want me to do about it?"

"It's what we *all* have to do about it. Your mom collects food for the needy every week and takes it down to church, right?"

"Yeah?"

"People need help, and she feels like she needs to help them, right?"

"Sure!"

"Well, if we really saw what we think we saw last night, and we can help some very sick people, don't you think we should do it? Don't you think it's kind of our responsibility?"

"Well sure, but how?"

Just then, Mary Fran pointed to where the trail comes out of the trees. Eli was pedaling up the path. "Hey, Eli!" she said when he got close to the house.

"Hey, Mary Fran," Eli replied as he came to a skidding halt. "Hey Josh, hey Mickey. What's going on?"

"Let's go inside for breakfast. Then we'll ride out to Big Oak. We can fill you in on the way."

I changed and we ate. After breakfast, as we pedaled out to Big Oak, Mary Fran and I explained what had happened at Mrs. Devitt's house. Eli accepted what we were telling him without hesitation, and Mickey was polite about not calling us bonkers.

"So what are we going to do?" Eli asked as we arrived at Big Oak.

"Well," I said, getting off my bike, "I was wondering if your mom still does the weekly church newsletter, you know, the one that lists the sick and housebound who would like prayers."

"Yeah?"

We all walked over to the little hill on Big Oak and sat down. I kicked at the multicolored tapestry of leaves on the little hill.

"Can you get us a copy of that?"

"Sure," Eli said, "what are we going to do?"

"What do you think! We're going to make them healthy and not housebound anymore."

"Okay. When do you want it?"

"Today. Right now."

"Oh come on! You couldn't have told me before I pedaled over here?"

"I didn't think of the newsletter until you were already on your way."

Eli's slumped posture and the look on his face told me that this explanation was not completely acceptable to him.

"Aw, now Eli, you know I wouldn't jerk you around like that. I'm telling you. Your mom's newsletter just popped into my head."

"It's a short ride, Eli," Mary Fran said as she picked up her bike. "Come on, I'll ride over with you."

That did the trick. His face lit up like the inside of an open refrigerator.

"Okay, in that case, I'll do it. But you know, if we're right and this *is* some sort of magic, healing water, this good deed is going to have people swarming all over this place. You wait 'til people find out!"

"I was wondering about that myself," Mary Fran said.

"Nobody's going to find out," I waved off their concern. "I

have a plan."

As the two of them pedaled off down the path, I tried to think up a plan.

CHAPTER THIRTY-FOUR

I Know You
(Told by Aggie)

Hello. Do you remember me? I'm the woman who's been swimming in Grout Brook. As I said before, I always try to be really careful about not going in there unless I can be sure I won't be caught. I can't afford to be chased out. But on that Saturday morning, I made a mistake. To be fair, I'd been up late the night before playing nursemaid to the stray dog who'd adopted me. She was giving birth to five puppies all of Friday night, and now it was Saturday morning and she and I were both exhausted. I shouldn't have gone to the brook that day, but the allure of the rejuvenating waters was too much to resist. I sat on a partially submerged flat rock, located in a part of the pool that gave me reasonably good cover, and rested my head on my rolled-up dress and towel. As I laid my head onto this makeshift pillow, I told myself that I shouldn't do it. I knew I was tired, and somewhere in the back of my mind, I knew that if I got comfortable, I would probably drift off to sleep naked. Not good.

It was the warmth of the mid-morning sun that finished me off.

I had gotten into the habit of swimming naked when Caleb

owned the place. He was the only one who ever came out to the brook and he was a perfect gentleman. He knew I swam naked and always warned me that he was approaching by whistling 'Oh! Susanna' as he came down the trail.

Also, I might have gotten a little too comfortable with my own nudity while attending a little music festival in August of 1969 called Woodstock. Perhaps I forgot that others aren't quite so at ease with the human body. Also, I'm pretty sure parents should be the ones to decide if that sort of free-thinking is appropriate for their children.

I woke up to the faint sound of an approaching discussion that was muted by the gurgling of the stream. Eyes still closed, I took about two seconds to inventory my circumstances. I was naked on a rock by the side of the stream, and I had an approaching audience.

The conversation stopped for several seconds, and I heard what was clearly the exclamation of a young boy.

"Holy smokes!"

I opened my eyes, saw a boy and a girl, both on bikes, each of whom I estimated to be between ten and twelve years old. I screeched as I pulled my clothes from beneath my head to cover my chest. I was mostly concerned with covering that area, as everything from the waist down was underwater … then I remembered how remarkably clear Grout Brook was. Thankfully, the young girl took charge.

"Eli, turn around!"

Eli, tore his gaze away from my nakedness for a moment to look at her, and only then seemed to realize that he still had that amazed-looking grin on his face.

"I wasn't looking," he said.

His eyes darted back to me. The girl, her fists balled up, stomped a foot and clenched her teeth. "Eli Morely!"

"Okay, okay already. I'm turning around."

He was not, and he did not … at least not until the girl slugged him in the shoulder. He then turned around. By then I'd recovered my wits, and my ability to speak.

"Thank you," I said, trying not to let them see how much the boy had amused me.

He'd turned his entire body away from me. After eyeballing him for a moment to be sure he didn't turn back around, the assertive young lady faced me again, then turned her eyes down to her feet.

"Sorry about that. Eli can be a goober, but he's okay once he remembers he's supposed to have manners."

I couldn't help smirking as I climbed out of the water, unrolled my towel and dried myself off. "Well, I know *his* name now. What's yours?"

"Mary Fran ma'am, I'm Mary Fran Barker, " she said with eyes still cast downward, "and I know who you are too."

I pulled my one-piece sundress over my head and was quickly dressed. "Oh really?"

"Yes ma'am, your name is Agnes Granger."

I didn't say anything ... I was stunned. I couldn't speak. How on Earth did she know my name? My face must have had the same slack-jawed look of astonishment that had been on Eli's face when he first saw me naked. Always wanting to draw as little attention to myself as possible, I tended to be a homebody and kept to myself, so I didn't have many acquaintances and would have remembered if I had met this precocious little girl before.

Finally, I managed to utter a few more words.

"Okay, I'm dressed now, and uhm ... have we met?"

Mary Fran looked up and sensed my discomfort.

"No, and you don't have to worry. Your secret is safe with us, we won't tell anybody."

I wondered which secret she was talking about, the fact that I was trespassing on Caleb's old property, or the fact that I was over 140 years old. I hoped it wasn't the latter. But how could she possibly know *that* secret?

"Secret?" I asked, smiling to try and hide my concern.

"You know, like how old you really are."

My heartbeat must have sounded like a jackhammer.

Be calm Aggie, be calm. Don't let her see the concern on your face.

Still smiling, I countered with a brilliant reply.

"What?"

"I saw an old picture of you. You were posing on a 1908

Model T in front of Granger's Drug Store and Soda Fountain."

Nobody had called the place by that name for decades. I was *really* rattled now. "Oh come on now ... what was your name again?"

"Mary Fran."

"Now Mary Fran, people have relatives and ancestors who look like them. That's what we call a family resemblance. And by the way, Agnes is very formal. You may call me Aggie."

"No, it's you Aggie. You both have that same birthmark on your neck." I must have looked like I'd seen a ghost. "But it's okay. You don't have to worry. We know all about Grout Brook, and we're not telling anybody."

"Then why did you even tell me that you knew who I was?"

The girl gestured with a finger that she wanted me to wait a moment. "Eli, you can turn back around now."

He did so, and tried unsuccessfully to hide his disappointment that I was now fully clothed. Mary Fran turned back to me. "I guess I just wanted to prove to myself that you really *were* the lady in the old picture."

I nodded. "So you know my secret. Now what?"

"That's why you come here, right?" the boy said, "because the water is what keeps you young, right?"

"Why? You *can't* keep me out. I *need* this water! I'll *die* without it."

"It's not our property Miss Aggie, and you're not gonna get kicked out," the little girl said.

"How can you be so sure if it's not your property?"

The boy answered me. "It's Josh's family's property. He's my best friend and he wants to help people with the water, not keep people away from it. That's what we're doing here now, Josh sent me back to my house to get the church newsletter ... so we can see who's sick, see who needs the water to get better."

"Well don't go telling everyone about the place. You'll have people from all over the planet in here."

"We know," the little girl said. "We already talked about that. We're gonna help folks in secret ... without them knowing how we did it."

"How many of you know about the water?" I asked.

"Four of us," Mary Fran, said, "if you count Mickey." My expression must have told her that more explanation was required, so she explained further, "Well, there's me and Eli here. Then there's Josh. Like Eli said, his folks own the place. Mickey goes to school with us." She pointed towards Nichols Corners Road. "He lives on the other side of the road over there."

"But Mickey doesn't believe the water has any powers," the boy added. "He thinks we're bonkers."

I couldn't help but like these kids, and I was even beginning to trust them a little too. I guess that's why I told them what I told them next. "Well, I guess I'm your proof for Mr. Mickey, huh?"

"I guess you are, Miss Aggie," the girl smiled as she spoke.

We said our goodbyes and the kids continued on their way. Then Mary Fran stopped and turned around to say one more thing. "Oh, Miss Aggie, ma'am?"

"Yes, sweetie?"

"Maybe you ought to swim in a bathing suit from now on, so the boys' eyes don't pop out of their heads."

CHAPTER THIRTY-FIVE

The Sick and Infirmed
(Told by Josh)

"It's about time," I said when Eli and Mary Fran came riding back up to the porch.

They came to the usual skidding stop, got off their bikes, and Eli handed me a piece of paper.

"Don't blame me. That naked lady was at Grout Brook again. Mary Fran just *had* to stop and gab with her."

Mary Fran rolled her eyes. "You know her *name* now, Eli. You can stop calling her that naked lady."

"You know her name?" I asked.

Mary Fran grinned like the cat who ate the bird, but she hadn't eaten the bird yet. I'd seen this look before and I knew, I was going to be the bird.

"Her name is Aggie, Aggie Granger!"

Aggie Granger, Aggie Granger, Aggie ... Granger.

My brain was on the freeway, but it was stuck in second gear. The name had left footprints in my mind at some point, but they weren't leading me anywhere. I knew I was the bird, and I thought I was going to be in the cat's mouth, I didn't realize I was already there.

I looked down at the sheet of paper. There were three names on it, and a way to change the subject while I searched my mind for the significance of the name Aggie Granger.

"Well, at least you guys got us the list. Let's go to the library and find out where these people live."

"I have a question," Eli announced, hands on hips. "Why don't we just ask one of our parents? They'd know where everyone on this list lives."

"They aren't stupid Eli. If we get them involved, they'll start asking questions." I folded the list and put it in my pocket, "Besides, they have enough to worry about. This isn't going to be easy, Eli. We need to try and help the people on the list without them realizing it was us and the water that helped them."

"Yeah," Mary Fran added, "if people find out what the water can do, they'll stampede Josh's farm."

"Well, how are we gonna do that?" Sometimes I wondered who tied Eli's shoes for him every morning, and based on the way Mary Fran was rolling her eyes, she was wondering the same thing.

Mickey, however, was a bit more patient. "I think we're gonna make tea, or lemonade, for them, something that uses water," he explained.

The light returned to Eli's eyes. The hamster was back on the wheel and running.

"Or soup?"

Eli had actually made a good suggestion. "Yeah, Eli. Soup's a good idea too."

* * *

There were two people in the library when we got there, Amy, and an elderly man who was reading the New York Times. Amy lit up like a Christmas tree when the soft jingle of the bell over the door announced our arrival.

"Well look who's here. If it isn't the four most wonderful kids in town. What are we up to today?"

Mary Fran was often our spokesperson, and this time was no different. "Hey Amy, how's Max doing?"

"Max is fit as a fiddle. Heck, he's wearing *me* out these days."

Eli chimed in. "Maybe we need to give *you* some of the – "

My elbow and Mary Fran's death glare hit Eli at the same time, reminding him to keep his frog mouth shut before he spilled the beans. As usual, Eli was a few laps behind the rest of us. He'd stopped talking, but seemed to have no idea what the problem was. Mary Fran gave a sideways twitch of her head toward the man reading the newspaper, and you could almost see that hamster slowly begin to start the wheel turning again.

Mickey grabbed the conversational steering wheel and directed the topic away from Eli before the dope could start talking again. I picked on Eli a lot, but truth be told, Mickey was really the only one of us boys who seemed to have a sufficient power supply to operate his brain and his mouth at the same time.

"Miss Amy," Mickey said, "can we talk someplace a little more private?" Amy took us back into the office behind the counter and left the door open just enough for her to see the front desk. Mickey continued. "Miss Amy, ma'am, we were wondering if you could help us find out where a few people in town live. They're on the sick and infirmed list at church. We thought it might be nice to call on them."

Now Amy was a little quicker of wit than Eli. For that matter, as much as we loved him, the stapler on Amy's desk was a little quicker of wit than Eli. But anyway, it seemed pretty clear that Amy knew exactly what we had in mind. She'd seen what the waters of Grout Brook had done for Max, and the gleam in her eyes told me that there was no need to lay out our plan in great detail.

"Well, the phone book can probably give you addresses. But I guess you need directions too, huh?"

"Yes ma'am," Mary Fran said.

"We have town and county maps over by the copier," Amy said, pointing to the back corner of the library. "How many names do you have?"

"Three," I said, handing the list to her.

"Maybe four," Mary Fran said.

Though we all looked at Mary Fran as if she were speaking Yiddish, it was Eli who asked the question.

"Four? Who's the fourth person?"

Mary Fran narrowed her eyes at him. "Have you forgotten Hannah Brady? Have you even noticed that she's been absent since school started back up? I guess my mamma's right when she says out of sight, out of mind."

Eli's eyes got as big as ping pong balls. "She's sick? I just figured she moved."

I wanted to keep quiet because I was another one who hadn't noticed that she was gone, but my mouth betrayed me.

"What is she sick with?"

"I don't know." Mary Fran's contempt melted into a worried look. "I asked Mrs. Harris, and she wouldn't tell me. But she looked like she was about to cry, so it's probably pretty bad."

CHAPTER THIRTY-SIX

Operation Downstream
(Told by Josh)

I was on the front porch at home when the other kids came pedaling out of the grove of trees that surrounded the path from Big Oak and Grout Brook. The smiles and enthusiastic chatter told me that they were as excited as I was to be doing this. As was typically the case, Mary Fran was out in front of Eli and Mickey by twenty or thirty feet, and was the first to get to the porch. She was off her bike and coming up the porch steps by the time the other two skidded to a stop, and she wasn't even out of breath.

"I can't believe your mom made soup for us to take around today," she said as she plopped down on the swing alarmingly close to me. "Did you make sure she used the right water?"

I scooched an inch to my left, which was as far away from her as I could scooch and still be on the swing. For a split-second, I was concerned about a sneak attack kiss, but normally she would only do this when no one else was around, and Eli and Mickey were almost right there.

"Yeah. I put the pan of water on the stove myself. Filled it up with the good water from downstairs."

"So, what's the plan?" Eli asked as he and Mickey came

140

bounding up the porch steps.

Now we'd gone over the plan in full detail last night as we rode our bikes home from the library and then again on this very porch, but I wasn't surprised at all that Eli asked to go over it again.

Mary Fran looked at me and grinned. She was pretty much past the eye-roll stage. Once you came to understand Eli's attention span, he became less exasperating. She smiled at him, stood up, and put a gentle hand on his shoulder. I could almost *see* the electricity crackle through his body when she touched him. He had it bad.

"We're all riding our bikes to Amy's house, in town. You and the other boys are going to visit the people who live right in the village. While you guys are doing that, Amy is going to take me to see Hannah Brady. She lives out of town. We'll meet up at Big Oak when we're done. Got it?"

"Yeah, uhm, I got it." Neither Eli's words nor his expression inspired confidence that he actually *did* have it, but it was okay, he'd be with me and Mickey.

I opened the door to let everyone inside as I spoke. "That was nice of Amy to offer to take you out to Hannah's house."

"Yeah, Hannah lives nine miles out," Mary Fran said. "Can you imagine how long it would have taken us to ride our bikes way out there!"

It was plain to see that Eli was proud that he was the one who suggested soup as a vehicle for delivery of the healing waters. "Is the soup ready?"

"Yep," I said, leading the gang into the kitchen. "Mom put it in four Tupperware containers." I opened the fridge and pulled the containers out, handing two to Eli and two to Mary Fran.

Eli took off his backpack and started to put his first two containers inside when Mary Fran stopped him.

"Hang on Eli," Mary Fran said. She put the two containers she was holding on the counter. "Josh, do you have any of those plastic bags they put your groceries in at the store?"

"Yeah," I said, pointing at a lower cupboard, "they're in there."

I was tying my sneakers while she got a bunch of bags out

and double wrapped each container. She handed three containers to Eli and looked around the kitchen and into what she could see of the living room from where she stood.

"Hey Josh, where's your folks?"

"Mom dropped me off after church and went back for some kind of meeting. Dad is where he always is, outside working on something."

Mary Fran snapped her fingers. "Hey, I almost forgot, can I fill a big soda bottle with the water downstairs?"

"Sure you can. You're not sick, are you?"

"Nah, it's for Amy. She called and asked if I could bring her some water when I came." My heart pounded harder for a moment, until Mary Fran continued. "She wants it for her friend, the lady who works in the town clerk's office next door to the library. I guess her friend's corgi is under the weather."

"What the heck is a Corgi?" I asked.

"It's a breed of dog, you goofball."

Eli chuckled as he hauled the backpack with the three containers of soup onto his back. He and Mickey headed out to the porch before I could put the extra shopping bags away and finish tying my sneakers. Mary Fran was back upstairs with the bottle of water by the time my shoes were tied. Finally, I stood up and started for the front door when Mary Fran raced past me and planted a kiss on my cheek. A 'run-by' kissing! Ugh! I ran out the front door just behind her and jumped on my bike.

"Hey! Wait up you goofballs."

CHAPTER THIRTY-SEVEN

Hannah Brady
(Told by Mary Fran)

After I wrapped the containers of soup in bags, I gave three of them to Eli and waited for him and Mickey to leave. After they left, I gave Josh a quick peck on the cheek. Then I took my container of soup outside, put it in my bicycle basket, and started up the driveway toward the road. Of course, it was a race. Halfway up the driveway, I was ahead of them all and looking back to see how much of a lead I had. Eli was the closest, about ten feet behind me. I put my head down and concentrated on my breathing. I wanted to go as hard as I could without getting winded. The key to winning the race that was always on when we rode our bikes anywhere, was to stay close enough to Josh and not get tired. I could beat him every time in a 100-yard sprint. If he got much farther ahead of me than that though, he'd usually win. As I expected, Eli passed me soon after we turned out of the driveway but I knew I'd be back in front of him before we were halfway there. I was never much worried about Eli, he had no idea how to pace himself.

When we got into town about twenty minutes later, I was in front of the pack. I turned my bike off the street and onto a triangular patch of grass not much bigger than the little league field. Morgan Bolt Park was dedicated to a local man who'd authored several bestselling fantasy novels and put our small town on the map. Three sidewalks connected the gazebo in the center to the corners of the sidewalk triangle that bordered the park. As I'd expected, it was Josh who got there next.

"I almost caught you," he said between heavy breaths. "I guess you had too much of a head start."

Now, I started about ten feet ahead of Josh and ended up thirty feet ahead of him, but I smiled, nodded, and let it go. Josh was a sweetheart.

"Yeah Josh, you'll probably get me next time, but those other two don't stand a chance."

This was enough to safeguard his ego, *and* we got to share a laugh at the expense of Mickey and Eli. To this day I still love those dimples of Josh's. The laughs faded, and we spent a few moments of silence that Josh seemed to find awkward before Mickey and Eli arrived.

"Here they come." I pointed north, where Mickey had just turned onto Maple St., followed shortly by Eli, who was clearly laboring. "Poor Eli looks like he's gonna drop."

Josh pointed out something that hadn't occurred to me. "He's too tall for that little bike. Those two should trade bikes. Mickey's too short for his bike, and Eli's too tall for *his*."

Mickey turned into Bolt park followed closely by poor, red-faced Eli, who got off the little bike and, hands on knees, tried to regain his breath. I glanced over at the bank clock on the other side of the park.

"Amy was expecting me five minutes ago, so I'm gonna ride down there now. You guys don't just run into people's houses, drop off soup, and run out," I instructed. "Introduce yourselves, tell them that you saw their name in the church bulletin. Try to actually get the soup into them. Sit down, talk to them for at least a few minutes, and *try* to act like you've been taught some manners."

I could feel the boys rolling their eyes behind me as I rode down the street toward Amy's, and that gave me great satisfaction. Boys could often act like savages who have not yet been taught how to live in civilized society.

When I got there, Amy was sitting on the steps that led up to her apartment above Clark's General store.

She stood up. "Hi, Mary Fran."

"Hi, Amy, sorry I'm late. We had to wait for Eli and Mickey. They can be a little slow on their bikes.

"That's okay. I was just enjoying the morning."

"Where's Max? Isn't he coming with us?"

"Oh no, honey. He's kind of big and he scares some people. We don't want to scare Hannah if she's already under the weather." She lifted my bike into the bed of her truck as she spoke. "Besides, dogs don't always get along with each other, and I didn't know if Hannah had a dog."

"She does," I said. "She showed me a picture of her dog once at school. Baby is a Chihuahua, and Hannah said sometimes she can be a little snot."

We both laughed as we climbed into the truck and closed the doors. On the way out to the Brady's house, I asked Amy how Max was doing and she bubbled over with joy.

"Maxey is as good as new," she said, as she shifted gears. "He's just like he was when he was a puppy. I hope I can get some of that water every now and then, just to keep him this way."

"Oh yes, ma'am. I'm *sure* that won't be a problem with Josh, and even if it *were* for some crazy reason, I'd get it for you myself."

Amy smiled. "Do you really think it can cure something as terrible as cancer in a *person*? I mean, in a dog is one thing but ..."

This jarred me. I hadn't known for sure that Hannah had cancer, but I guess deep down, I suspected it. At school, no one had actually said the word, they just told us she was ill, but we all kind of knew that she wasn't getting any better. As a child however, you never want to surrender hope.

"Oh, yes ma'am. I know somebody who had a sickness that has *never* been cured." Aging, I reasoned, had never been cured. "The water cured that. But I can't tell you who it is. I promised to keep *that* a secret."

Amy started to say something, but she stopped herself and we rode the rest of the way in silence. At the Brady's house, we parked behind the town police car in the driveway and Amy came to the door with me. We knocked and Mr. Brady answered quickly. I was awed by how tall and imposing he looked standing there in his police uniform. His expression was one of disappointment, as if he'd been expecting someone else.

"Hello, Officer Brady."

"That's Chief Brady."

"Oh, I'm sorry, Chief. My name is Mary Fran Barker. I'm the girl who called yesterday about stopping in to visit with Hannah." He looked at me briefly and then turned his attention to Amy.

His eyes asked the next question. I smiled a nervous smile and answered that unspoken question.

"This is my friend Amy. She's the librarian in town. She was nice enough to give me a ride out here. I didn't think it would be polite to ask her to wait in her truck."

Brady nodded. Amy smiled and nodded back. "Nice to meet you, Chief Brady."

His expression didn't change. He grunted in response, took a step back and opened the door to let us in. The house wasn't filthy, but you could tell that there wasn't a woman living there. No pictures, no decorative touches. There were shades, which were drawn, but no curtains. Brady led us into the living room where the feeble girl was curled up on the sofa with her little tan dog. Baby jumped off the sofa with a single defiant bark and ran to her bed in the corner of the room.

The way Hannah's jet black hair framed her drawn face had me immediately fighting back tears. It reminded me of something I'd once heard my momma say. This poor girl truly *did* have one foot in the grave and the other on a banana peel. Hannah's blanket was clean, but it wasn't a blanket for a sick little girl. It looked more like an old Army blanket, and just looking at it made me itch all over.

"Hannah, these folks are from the church in town. They heard you weren't feeling well and came to visit with you for a bit. You keep an eye out for Miss Kate and call me if you see her coming. Okay?"

"Okay Daddy," Hannah said in a tiny voice. She picked up

the remote, muted the TV, and turned to us. "Hi, Mary Fran."

"Hi, Hannah, this is my friend Amy. We thought that with you being sick and all, you probably don't get out much and might like some company."

"Hi, Hannah," Amy said, stepping forward and setting some books on the coffee table. "I brought some books I thought you might like. I hope you don't mind that I checked them out to your library card."

"Amy's the librarian in town," I explained.

Hannah smiled. "Hi, Amy. I don't mind, thank you for bringing them. It's just that I don't know how I'm going to be able to return them."

"Don't you worry about that. You can call me at the library when you're done with them and I'll come and pick these up and bring you some more."

"You guys should sit down. You'll get tired standing there."

I started to sit, but I saw her father peeking in on us and took the opportunity to talk to him. "Chief Brady, my friend's mom made soup for Hannah, is it okay if I warm some up for her?"

He nodded to his right, "The kitchen is right this way."

In the kitchen, I took the soup out of the plastic grocery bags and poured it into a small saucepan. While it warmed up, I tossed the grocery bags in the trash and took a bowl and spoon out of the dish rack on the counter. I couldn't help seeing the medical bills on the table and saw dollar figures that literally startled me. At eleven, I had no idea that human beings would charge each other such terrible amounts to keep them alive. When the soup began to bubble and steam, I poured it into the bowl and brought it into the living room with the spoon and a paper towel. Hannah was now sitting up and Amy was telling her about one of the books she'd brought.

"Here you go, Hannah. My friend's mom made this soup. It'll make you feel better."

For the next five to ten minutes we sat with Hannah and talked about the books Amy had brought, the other kids at school, and the lessons she'd missed. I eyeballed her all the while, making sure she was eating the soup and looking for any improvement in her appearance. Meanwhile, Amy made friends with Baby and watched out the window. "Mary Fran," she said, "it looks like someone is here. We better get going."

"Okay Amy," I said, eyeballing Hannah as we walked toward the door.

Hannah took a few more spoonfuls of soup and Amy shouted up the stairs as we reached the front door.

"Chief Brady, it looks like the person you're waiting for is here. We're leaving now. Thank you very much for letting us visit with Hannah."

I kept my eyes on Hannah as we left. She was still eating soup.

As Amy drove me back toward Josh's, I asked her to stop and let me out on Nichols Corners Road. The spot looked like it was in the middle of nowhere. She *did* slow to a stop, but protested.

"Now why on Earth would I let you out here?"

We were stopped, but the truck was still in drive. I pointed to an opening in the roadside trees to our right. "That path in the woods leads to a place that me and the boys call Big Oak. That's where we're meeting when we get back. It's actually just a spot on the edge of the woods where we sit under this big, ole' oak tree. From here, it's about a hundred-fifty feet into the woods. If you drive me all the way around to Josh's house, then it's about two football fields to get back to Big Oak." Amy was skeptical, and we went back and forth for a few minutes. Eventually, I lobbed one last argument at her. "It's the path to and from my house. That's my mailbox we just passed." I pointed to the blue mailbox fifty yards behind the truck. "We ride this path on our bikes all the time."

"Well ..." she said, and finally put the truck in park, "I *guess* if you use this path all the time ..." she never finished the sentence, but she got out and helped me get my bike out of the back of the truck. We waved to each other as I rode up the trail.

"Be careful, Mary Fran."

CHAPTER THIRTY-EIGHT

The Shortcut
(Told by Mary Fran)

When going up the wooded trail from Nichols Corners Road, you can take the left-hand trail before you get to Big Oak, and come to Grout Brook. My bike was fairly new and wasn't as loud as Eli's, so as I neared Grout Brook, the gurgling of water over the rocks was loud enough that I surprised Miss Aggie at the deep hole.

"Hey, Miss Aggie."

She straightened up and jerked her head around. "Oh dear! Mary Fran, you startled me."

"I'm sorry ma'am, I didn't mean to scare you. That's a really pretty bathing suit you have on."

She smiled at me. "Well, we don't want the boys' eyes popping out now, do we? Where are the boys anyway? Usually if I see one of you, I see all of you."

"I'm going to meet them now, just up the trail some. We were out helping sick folks with the water." I saw her face fall. "Oh, don't worry Miss Aggie, we didn't *tell* anybody about the water. We brought them soup that Josh's mom made with it. *She* doesn't even know the water is special."

She sighed and smiled at me. "That was nice. You kids are sweet. I bet that was quite a chore."

"Nah, it wasn't too bad. We rode our bikes into town together. Then the boys went to see the three people in town, and I got a ride from town to the Brady's house. They live a few miles out."

Something I said made Miss Aggie's expression go sour. "The Bradys? What Bradys? Where do they live?"

"Hannah Brady ma'am," I couldn't hide the concern in my *own* voice. I didn't know what I'd said, and I didn't want to upset her any further. "Well, Hannah and her daddy. She goes to our school. Or she *did* go to our school, until she got sick. She hasn't been in school for quite a spell now. They live out on Shaleumeth Hill Road. Her daddy's the police chief."

"How do you know he's the police chief?"

"Hannah told me. Besides, he was getting ready to go to work when we got there, and Miss Amy parked right behind his police car. I called him Officer Brady by mistake and he corrected me, told me it was Chief Brady."

"Yeah, that sounds like him. Did anything about him stand out?"

"Yes, ma'am. He's a really big man. He's gotta be the tallest man I ever saw. He's like a giant."

It was true. He was the tallest man I'd ever seen to that point in my young life. At six feet eight inches, he might still, all these years later, be the tallest man I've ever met in person.

Miss Aggie paused, looking up as if to try to pull an answer out of the air, like most of us do when we're thinking.

"Maybe you shouldn't go out there anymore."

I was baffled. Something about me going to Hannah's really set Miss Aggie off.

"What's the matter? Hannah and her daddy were really nice."

Now that was a small fib. Mr. Brady wasn't exactly nice. He wasn't mean or anything, but he wasn't exactly welcoming either. But my mother had always taught me not to speak ill of other folks. She always said that if you can't say anything nice about someone, you shouldn't say anything at all. So yeah, I told a little white lie.

"Just the same," Miss Aggie said, "maybe you should have an adult help out with Hannah."

"I did. Like I told you, Miss Amy was there. She went in with me and visited, and everything was okay." I gave her my most reassuring smile, "So there wasn't no reason to worry."

"Well … okay." She scrunched her brow up a little bit when she said it. I could tell she still wasn't completely convinced, but she let it go. We said our goodbyes, I got back on my bike, waved, and pedaled off, up the path toward Big Oak. I wondered why she was so concerned. I mean my momma taught me about there being bad people out there, but this was a police officer. He was one of the men who *protected* us from bad people.

When Big Oak came into view, the boys were looking the other way, up the other trail, towards Josh's house. I guess they were expecting me to be coming from that direction, so I called out to them.

"Hey, guys. How'd it go?"

They all turned toward me, and Eli and Mickey waved, but Josh's reaction caught me off guard. He jumped to his feet and took a couple of steps towards me. The other two boys couldn't see his face but I could. He wasn't exactly mad … but he wasn't happy either. His eyes showed concern, and his mouth, displeasure. Mickey and Eli started to talk, but Josh snapped at me over both of them.

"What do you mean, how'd it go? I thought you got hit by a car or something."

The other two boys stopped talking and their jaws fell open. We all just stared at him. *They* were in shock, and I was a little bit deeper in love. He was *worried* about me!

CHAPTER THIRTY-NINE

Meeting Jennifer Corey
(Told by Amy)

As I drove back towards town on Nichols Corners Road, I passed a white car in the 'pull-off' parking area, and farther down the road, a large blue car was pulled off the side of the road, and turned onto Deleon Road. I noticed this because it was unusual to see one car on Nichols Corners Road, let alone two cars off the side of the road. As I got closer to town, I grew more and more uncomfortable about having let Mary Fran out of my truck to go pedaling up that forest trail. The truth is, I'd been preoccupied. There had been something tapping at my thoughts from my subconscious. Have you ever had the feeling that you were forgetting to do something or missing something, but been unable to figure out what it was? That something was bothering me so much when I let Mary Fran out, that I hadn't used my best judgment. But the whole way back to town, I thought about the blue car I'd passed and that little girl, riding her bike alone through those woods. Whose car was that? Was the owner of that car *in* those woods? My worry was like a light dusting of snow at first, and it was the equivalent of a waist deep, driving blizzard by the time I got back to my apartment.

That car could have belonged to anyone, could have been a madman's car. I thought as I stroked Max on his head.

I stood there, thinking about it for a few seconds. Max seemed to know what I was thinking. He looked up at me as if to say, 'Well? What are you going to do about it?'

"Max, stop looking at me like that," I half demanded and half begged. Then I gave in. "Okay, let's go, boy."

His tail wagged faster, and he followed me down the stairs and into my truck. He licked my face as I put the truck in reverse, backed it out the driveway, and headed out to the Corey's place. I had to go back, and make sure nothing horrible had befallen Mary Fran on her ride through the woods. As I drove, in an effort to keep my worry about Mary Fran at bay, I went back to trying to reach the unseen thing that had been tapping at the underside of my conscious thoughts. What *was* it that I was supposed to know or remember?

But even now that I'd made up my mind to go back and check on Mary Fran, I still couldn't go back and find this elusive bit of information. A new impediment was blocking my train of thought. If I was *not* insane, and Max's miraculous recovery *was* caused by what I thought it was, then there was a river of healing waters and eternal life running through our little town. I was busy imagining how this could affect everyone here.

As I drove out of town on DeLeon Road, my attention darted to my right for an instant. In the passenger seat, Max sat and watched me drive. It might seem odd to some people that a dog wouldn't be looking out the window, but not to me. Until the day I took him home, he'd known little but a concrete cell with a metal door. Now that he had a home and a person, he seemed deathly afraid of losing both. Every day, when I came home, he'd be at the door, tail wagging, and the blanket next to the door would be warm to the touch … as if he had been lying there for some time. When I wasn't at work, he insisted on being right beside me, everywhere, and all the time. Having him stare at me as I drove was normal. He always did this, and I understood. He'd already been taken to the shelter and left there twice. He was probably worried that it would happen again. Sweet baby, could you blame him?

Eyes back on the road, my mind returned to Grout Brook. What might a river of healing waters look like? I thought about Caleb Hanley, wondering again if he really *could* have been over 145 years old when he died. When I first saw it in the county documents, I considered the possibility for about as long as it takes to sneeze, and dismissed it without any further thought. But then there was Dr. Markle. When she called me back in and told me that Max's X-rays were clear, that he was cancer free, and she had no clue how that happened, I certainly had a clue. If the water cured every sickness, why *couldn't* you live forever? I gave this more than a moment's thought. In fact, as I turned into the Corey driveway, I was still thinking about it.

A few yards down the driveway, when we crossed an old bridge of wooden beams that spanned a small stream, I wondered about this little trickle of water.

Could this possibly be ... no way. I could jump across that tiny stream.

What I almost missed was Max. He wasn't watching me anymore. He had his nose up to the partially open window and was sniffing like he'd never experienced farm air before. Maybe he hadn't. I eased the truck to a stop behind a monstrosity of a station wagon that was parked in front of the house. I got out and went around the truck to let Max out. When I opened the passenger door, he leapt from the truck and took off towards a grove of trees, a hundred yards off the right side of the house. This was the first time he'd ever run from me like that. He normally preferred to stay lodged up my butt like ill-fitting jeans.

"Max no! Max, you get *back* here." Though I yelled, I was suppressing a smirk.

Just then, a woman came out the front door of the house and down the porch steps. She was slender with wavy, shoulder length hair that was in the best place between brunette and redhead. Her sparkling brown eyes made me more than a little jealous.

"Hi," she said, extending a hand, "you must be Amy."

She was as pleasant as her smile, and while her knee-length, smock dress and the dishcloth on her shoulder said housewife, her statuesque height, sultry voice and everything else

154

about her screamed Hollywood. I took her hand and we shook, but I was a bit baffled.

"How ... uhm ... I mean hi. But how did you ..."

She laughed. "I saw you pull up through the window, *and*, I saw your dog take off."

I looked in the direction Max had gone. "My dog?"

"Oh yeah! That's *got* to be Max. Josh told me everything about Max. Those kids love that dog!"

My ego clattered to the ground. The kids hadn't told her about me. It was my dog who'd made an impression! "Yeah, that's Max." I was looking back and forth between Mrs. Corey and the woods where Max had vanished. "He's quite a character. He loves the kids too."

"Would you like to come in for coffee?"

"Oh no, Mrs. Corey. I just stopped because I dropped Mary Fran off at a trail over on Nichols Corners Road and I was having second thoughts about that. She said it was a shorter ride from there up the trail to some place she wanted to meet the boys. Some place by an oak tree, or something."

"Oh yeah, Big Oak, that's one of their favorite spots."

I smiled. "Yes, that was the place she said. But anyway, I just didn't feel right leaving her to pedal through the woods. Would it be okay if I went down to be sure she got there okay?"

"Oh, yeah. It's right down that trail," she pointed in the direction that Max had run off, "my bike's over in the barn. You can use it to ride down there if you like."

"Oh, no thank you. I also have a runaway dog to corral."

"Okay," she pointed, "if you just stay on that trail, you can't miss them."

"Thank you very much."

"If you get back to your truck and change your mind about that cup of coffee, just knock."

After smiles and quick, polite goodbye waves, she went back inside to her domestic domain, and I jogged off towards the trail in the trees.

CHAPTER FORTY

Pups At Play
(Told by Josh)

Mickey, Eli, and I had been back at Big Oak for about half an hour, and I was beginning to worry about Mary Fran. Where the heck was she? *We'd* visited three people and she'd only gone to see Hannah Brady. I was watching up the trail that leads to the house when Mary Fran came pedaling up from the other direction, she was on the trail from Grout Brook.

"Hey, guys. How'd it go?"

I surprised myself with my reaction. "What do you mean, how'd it go? I thought you got hit by a car or something!"

When Mary Fran and the other two went quiet, it hit me. They were all staring at me. Maybe I'd let a little too much slip out. Her lips twitched up at the corners for just a second, a quick smile. I understood that this bit of worry I'd let slip out had betrayed me, misrepresented me. Mary Fran now knew I cared about her. I guess that was when I realized it too. The problem was, neither of us really understood exactly *how* I cared about her. My heart belonged to Amy, but I was truly worried about Mary Fran that day. I guess that's how guys who have them, love their sisters. The problem was, I didn't have a sister, and at age eleven, I didn't have a firm grasp on the difference. Based on the three stupid grins I was looking at, neither did Eli, Mary Fran, or Mickey.

Mary Fran's dumb expression was more concerning than the other two. Hers had the terrifying look of infatuation. We all stood there looking at each other like idiots for a few seconds that felt like an hour.

Mary Fran finally broke the silence. "How long have you guys been back?"

"Maybe a half an hour," Mickey said.

"How'd you guys get back so fast? Did you boys make sure your sick folks actually ate some of the soup?"

"Sure did," Eli said with his chest puffed out.

I was never happier to have Eli take charge. I was still regrouping, and mentally kicking myself for having given Mary Fran the wrong idea.

Unsatisfied with Eli's reassurance, Mary Fran asked again. "You guys had three people to visit. How the heck did you get back so fast?"

Eli rolled his eyes and shocked me with what, for him, qualified as razor-sharp wit. "Duh! We had three people to visit and there are three of us!"

Mary Fran was apparently stunned as well. She was rendered speechless, a condition that *rarely* afflicted her, I'm talking *Haley's Comet* rare.

So there we stood without any words; me still concerned about the amorous glint I'd seen in Mary Fran's eyes, Mary Fran and Mickey stunned by Eli's spasm of wit, and Eli chest out, proud of having bested Little Miss Knows-Everything. God only knows how long we might have stood there if Penny and Max hadn't come tearing down the trail from home.

Mickey and I screamed in unison. "Max!"

Of course, the dogs ran to Mary Fran. She got down onto one knee to greet them. I swear she rubs bacon on her hands before she comes out, just so she can gloat about how all the dogs like her better. She never says anything, but she gloats with that annoying, *they like me better*, look. I *know* that's what she's thinking!

"Hi, Penny. *Hey*, Max." She petted both dogs enthusiastically. "What are you doing here? You didn't run away from Amy, did you?"

"No honey." I knew that voice behind me. It was *Amy*. My knees melted a little, and threatened to buckle. We all turned around. "Max and I were worried. We just came back to make sure you got up that trail in the woods okay."

I hadn't known that Amy wore shorts. For an eleven-year-old boy, this was a significant piece of information, and I approved.

"Aw, you didn't have to do that. I told you, we use that trail all the time. Don't we guys?"

We were all mute, but for a different reason now. All I knew at the moment was that I liked Amy, and I liked those shorts. At eleven, I wasn't completely sure *why*. In a few years, I'd gain a more precise understanding of why Amy always robbed us boys of our ability to speak.

"Guys … guys?" Mary Fran poked at us verbally. "*Guys!*"

Mickey snapped out of it first. "Oh uhm, yeah, she's right. All of us except Josh live on Nichols Corners Road, this is the shortcut to his house."

Mary Fran approved of his answer. I could tell because the scowl on her face melted. Just when I thought all was well, the dogs bolted.

I yelled at them. "Hey!" Mary Fran shrieked, and we all jumped up to chase them down the trail to Grout Brook.

We could have walked. The dogs weren't running from us, they were running to the water. When we caught up to them, they were playing in the brook like a couple of puppies. The scene seemed to overwhelm Amy, the two dogs playing in the brilliant blue waters of a stream three times the width of the average driveway, and the droplets they splashed glistening in the brilliant sun. She was the one standing there mute now. The look on her face seemed to say, 'So this is the magical Grout Brook.'

It took me a while to realize that she was trembling. I didn't understand. On this beautiful, sun-soaked, autumn day, Amy was standing there, watching the dogs, and trembling.

CHAPTER FORTY-ONE

It's a Bet
(Told by Josh)

Eventually, we fell into a routine. It wasn't tedium. There's a difference. We enjoyed what we were doing. Eli brought us the list of sick and infirmed from the church bulletin each Friday, and Mary Fran took the list to the library and used the maps to plan our Sunday itinerary. Often, we went with her. Though they knew nothing about Grout Brook, Mary Fran's mom and my mom were so impressed with what we were doing, that they volunteered to provide car rides for out of town people.

Word traveled fast, and as more and more people seemed to benefit from our visits, our list gradually grew. We got into the habit of ending our visits with a prayer. Since these names came off a church list, the people already believed in prayer. It wasn't that we *didn't*. But if they thought they were healed by the power of prayer, that would keep them from wondering what *did* heal them and nosing around Grout Brook. This was Mary Fran's brilliant idea. But I'll never admit I said that.

Mom and Dad were thrilled that I'd begun to show more urgency with regard to my studies. I knew my Sundays were going to be occupied with visits to sick people. I also knew that if my

159

grades weren't good, Mom and Dad would put an end to my civic efforts, so when I got home on Friday nights, I got right to my schoolwork. Heck, I even began to study in study hall.

On one Saturday in early November, when I was sitting on the front porch memorizing two pages of American history, I heard the front door open behind me but I didn't turn around. I was too deeply immersed in the sequence of historical events that led up to the formation of the United States. When Mom spoke, however, I came out of my educational trance.

"Josh honey, sorry to interrupt you, but I just wanted to tell you how proud your father and I are of the way you've grown."

I was perplexed. "I have? My clothes still fit me just fine."

She laughed. "No sweetie, not like that. I mean you've grown emotionally. You've become more mature. You've become community-minded, helping others, and you are so attentive to your studies now. We couldn't be any more proud of you than we are right now."

"Oh, thanks," I said. I didn't feel all of that change happening. I just knew it felt good to help people, and like I said earlier, my parents wouldn't let me continue to do it if my grades went down. But it did feel good to hear Mom say all that nice stuff. "Anything else?"

"Yeah," she said from behind the dreaded *Mom smile*. Here it came. "I was thinking if you want, you could invite Mary Fran over for dinner."

There it was! That was the other shoe. It was nice that my parents were thrilled with what they perceived as my transformation, but there was a downside. Mom was under the impression that some or all of this transformation was a direct result of my association with Mary Fran, and I feared that she meant to extend that association in a permanent, husband and wife manner. *That*, I found to be an unsettling prospect, to say the least.

"Sure Mom, the gang's coming over this afternoon. I told them to be over around five." Mom's smile flickered to a frown then back to a smile. She hadn't invited *the gang*, she invited *Mary Fran*.

"Okay, good. I'll set three extra places," she said with considerably less music in her voice. We gave each other the side-eye and she went back inside.

Mom hadn't been inside ten minutes when the shuffle of approaching footsteps made me look up.

"Hey Mickey, what are you walking for? Where's your bike?"

"Flat tire," he said, mindlessly flipping a dirty old coin.

I folded my study notes and stood up. "You want me to come over and help you patch it?"

"Nah. Mom's taking it down to the gas station. She dropped me off on the way."

"Great, then you can make yourself useful. Here," I said, holding out my study notes, "you can quiz me on these American History dates."

Mickey put the coin in his pocket, took my notes, and we went out to the barn. I don't know how true it is, but I firmly believed that one could coax information from one's brain more easily when jumping from one hay bale to another. My memory proved to be good, but not perfect. I only got three out of twenty dates wrong. The problem was, three wrong was *not* good enough for me anymore.

"One more time, Mickey. I'll get 'em all right this time."

"Since when do you have to get them *all* right?"

It was a good question. Before, I'd always been happy with B's and C's, but Mom's little 'attaboy' earlier had triggered something more in me. I liked it when Mom and Dad were proud of me.

"You just never mind that and quiz me one more time."

Then he went and did it. Mickey had to have the last word. "Who do you think you are, Mary Fran?"

That was it. He'd pushed me too far and I shot him a look. "I'll bet you that silver dollar you just put in your pocket that I get 'em all right this time."

"It's a bet!"

CHAPTER FORTY-TWO

Unhook That Cow

(Told by Josh)

That Sunday would prove to hold an unexpected surprise. The plan was that after church and our visits, we would all meet at Big Oak like we always did. Church let out ten minutes later than usual and we had more visits than normal. So when we finished with the visits, I was trying to make up for lost time. I was sure Mary Fran, Eli, and Mickey were as well.

We had agreed to get changed and meet at Big Oak just as soon as we could. On the way back from visiting sick people, we all pedaled like mad down my driveway. Everyone would change into play clothes and be on their way to Big Oak within minutes. While I dropped my bike and hurried up the front steps, Mary Fran, Eli, and Mickey veered right, and headed down the trail. I had the advantage because I was home and changing first ... or so I thought. Mom, you see, couldn't understand what the big hurry was. I was beginning to seriously believe that mothers got some sort of secret reward when they found out their kids were in a hurry to get somewhere, and could tie an anchor to their pants. When I went in the front door she was lying in wait.

"Josh honey, is that you?" came the deceptively melodic words from the kitchen.

Her voice had the tone of a woman who had a piece of fresh-baked pie for her son. The reality was that she was a crocodile, just beneath the surface, nothing but eyes and nostrils visible … waiting for some unsuspecting schlep of a zebra to come in close for a drink.

"Yeah Mom," I said.

For the uninitiated, I was the zebra.

"I know you're planning to go out and play with your friends, but do you think you can do me a few small favors before you go?"

A few small favors?

The crocodile had lunged and had the hapless zebra by the leg. The poor, stupid beast was thrashing and braying, but his fate was sealed.

"What do you want me to do, Mom?" The croc was pulling the zebra under.

"Could you take the clothes in off the line? I wouldn't normally ask you to do that for me, but –" I cut her off in my mind.

But you thought I might go down to Big Oak and have fun? We can't have that, can we?

"... it looks like it could rain" she finished, unaware of my silent interruption. "Also could you bring the dog food in from the car and pour it in Penny's food bin?"

The sucking sound you heard was my remaining daylight circling the drain. As if losing my fun time wasn't bad enough, I was being kept from Big Oak by *girl's* work! I, of course, knew better than to say that to Mom. Because as far as I knew, no dead eleven-year-old boy had ever gone to hang out with his friends.

Dog food detail seemed to be the quicker of the two tasks and I desperately wanted to be half-done … even if the first half took five minutes and the second half would take twenty minutes. I could still plausibly convince my kid-mind that I was half done.

As expected, the dog food transfer was relatively quick, and I found myself out back, taking down laundry, and imagining Eli, Mickey, and Mary Fran having fun without me.

It was not lost on me that they never seemed to come by when Mom had chores for me. But if Mom had pie in there waiting for me, those yahoos would have had some reason to come over before they went to their houses. I grumbled as I took down laundry with visions of the others relaxing in the shade of Big Oak without me.

I don't know what rain Mom was forecasting, but it was good that she already had a job being Mom. She sure didn't have a future as a weather forecaster. The clouds passed, the afternoon sun was high, and as I expected, the others were all lying in the shade of Big Oak, waiting to make fun of me when I got there.

I braced for the barrage of smart-aleck remarks, and the other kids didn't disappoint me. "Hey, guys."

"Whoa, it's The Flash!"

"Very funny, Eli." Eli didn't often get to be snarky about beating me in a bike race, so I was going to let that go, but Mary Fran ...

"Gee whiz, Josh, it's a good thing my life doesn't ever depend on you getting someplace fast." A crow cawed, and sounded like it was laughing.

"Big talk for a girl who I beat half the time we race anywhere."

She smiled an impish grin. "But not *this* time."

"Aw, come on guys, my mom had chores for me to do."

"Josh," she said with hands on hips, "I went home, changed clothes, made a sandwich, ate the sandwich, drank a glass of tea, and I *still* beat you here by four minutes."

Mickey and Eli rolled on the ground laughing and I'd had just about enough. I stood up and put my baseball cap on the ground upside down. "Okay, everybody up and on your bikes. We're racing to my house, around my driveway circle, and back here. Last one back puts a buck in here, second to last back puts in fifty cents, and the second place finisher puts in a quarter. Winner takes the pot. We start on my countdown from three."

"Why do I have to race?" Mickey protested. "I didn't say anything."

"No, but when Mary Fran cracked wise, you and Eli were rolling around on the ground, cackling like a couple of her chickens. Now get on your bikes smart-alecks!"

My plan to shut them all up backfired when Mary Fran got back to Big Oak first with time to think up a good wisecrack, which she dropped on me fifty-two seconds after finishing … according to her watch.

"Glad to see you made it back, Josh, I would have organized a search party to find you, but I was the only one here."

I would have hit her with some genius comeback if I'd actually *had* a genius comeback. It turns out though, that all I had was a jealous scowl and a need to get more air in my lungs. Still gasping for air, I disdainfully tossed my quarter in the hat and picked the hat up. At least I'd be able to shut Mickey and Eli up.

I was holding the hat out, upside down by the bill thirty-three seconds later, when Eli came huffing and puffing down the trail.

"Pay up, speedy, fifty cents American."

Eli gave me the same annoyed scowl I'd given Mary Fran, so at least I'd gotten back at *him*.

Poor Mickey, with those short little legs was last, and if you think my experience getting picked on minutes ago gave me any sort of sympathy … you don't understand the kid rules. Someone had to pay.

Mickey was still twenty feet away when I yelled, "Mickey, next time we race I'll put blocks on your pedals to make it fair."

Eli went the safe route and copied the insult I'd used on him. He didn't have to think this way. "Pay up, speedy, one dollar American."

Mary Fran and I just stared at Eli with a 'can't-you-think-up-your-own-insults?' kind of look.

"Don't pay attention to those two Mickey, they lost too," Mary Fran smirked and went on in a deadpan voice, "now unhook that cow you were draggin' behind your bike, put a dollar in the hat, and sit down."

She was even better than me at *insults*. Sometimes Mary Fran was really annoying.

"Hey!" Eli said, holding up a dirty old coin, "look what I found."

"Can I see it?" I asked him.

Eli handed the coin over and I inspected it. "This is just like the one Mickey found earlier today. Hey Mickey, look at this."

Mickey came over to where I was sitting to have a look. He reached into the baseball cap, pulled out the coin he'd just put inside, and held it next to Eli's for both of us to compare.

"Yep!" I said, "They're exactly the same. Where'd you find this, Eli?"

Eli pointed to a spot about thirty feet away. "Right over there. By where that big old milk can used to be. Where'd that go anyway?"

"It's in the barn. Mom wanted Dad to pull it out of the ground, clean it up, and repaint it. She wants to mount the mailbox on it."

Mickey looked at me with a strange expression and said, "That's where I found *my* coin too."

Mary Fran scrambled to her feet and hurried over to the place Eli had indicated. She dropped to her knees and started digging into a three square foot area of disturbed soil.

"Found one," she said, raising her find triumphantly before stuffing it in her pocket and going back to digging. Mickey, Eli, and I all looked at each other and jumped to our feet, but before we could get over there, Mary Fran sounded off again. "'Nuther one."

We unearthed five more of the dirty old coins in the next hour, all of them the same. When we were pretty sure we had found all of the coins that would be easy to find, we modified the plan. Mary Fran would ride into town with her mom tomorrow, bring one of the coins into the antique shop, and find out what it was worth. Then she'd meet us boys back here with tools to dig with, and see if we could find any more.

CHAPTER FORTY-THREE

Blue Treasures
(Told by Josh)

The conversation at dinner that night started out fairly normal. Dad told us what he had to get done on the farm in the coming week and Mom asked me how our day went after church.

"We had seven people to visit today if you count Mrs. Devitt."

"Why wouldn't you count Mrs. Devitt?" Dad asked.

"Well, she seems to be doing pretty well, and she says she isn't sick anymore. Says she's felt great since that night last month. But we like to check in on her anyway. She's kind of special to us."

Mom smiled. "Yeah. She's been doing pretty well for almost a month now. I hear she's even started baking pies again. Are you sure the reason you guys keep checking in on her is to be sure she's okay?"

I gave Mom my most offended look. "What? You think we're going to see Mrs. Devitt just for *pie*?"

"No," she said with her favorite smirk, "not *just* for pie. But I suspect that pie *is* a factor."

We hadn't even *had* any pie. Mrs. Devitt made us *cupcakes* that day! I glared at Mom, rolled my eyes, and changed the subject. "Hey Mom, if we find the treasure, how much of it can we keep?"

Her expression flickered. For a half a second, I saw the same look on her face that I usually saw when she was worried. Then she smiled, shot a sideways glance at Dad and he answered my question.

"Why wouldn't you be able to keep it all?" Mom gave him the side-eye again. He swallowed his last bite of meatloaf, fought back a grin, but didn't say anything more.

She'd said it before, and now she was saying it again with her eyes. She was worried about us being disappointed when we found that there was no treasure. They had no faith in us. They didn't think we'd find any treasure, and we'd found *two*. I wanted so badly to tell them about what we'd found, but I didn't know if there were more gold coins in that spot or not. When we knew how much we had, we'd cut it up into four equal parts. After we knew all of that, I could tell Mom and Dad. If I told them now, there would be a lot of questions that I couldn't answer yet.

"Are you sure?"

"Absolutely son," Dad said, "this is your farm too. And you're the only one of us who showed the initiative to hunt for treasure. So if you find it, it's all yours."

The twinge of guilt returned. I felt like I should tell them, right then and there, what we'd already found.

Later that night, while Mom and Dad were in the kitchen doing dishes, I overheard them talking about me and my treasure hunt.

"I don't know. I worry that encouraging him like this is just setting him up for disappointment when he doesn't find any treasure."

I eased closer to the entrance to the kitchen and peeked around the corner.

"Jennifer, being an adult is nothing *but* disappointment after disappointment. He's going to have to learn to deal with it eventually. Besides, when I was a kid, I used to go treasure hunting all the time."

"Oh yeah? Ever find any treasure?"

Dad put the pan he was drying in the cabinet, slung the dish towel over his shoulder, took Mom by her waist, and pulled her in close to him.

"I found you."

Oh God! My dinner was going to come back up like a Saturn rocket.

Mom giggled like Mary Fran, and hugged him. It reminded me of the hug Amy gave *me* in the store. It wasn't the same *kind* of hug, but it was a hug, and this was different. These were my *parents* … ugh!

They kissed, and Mom looked up at Dad all moon-eyed. "No really, what was the best treasure you ever found?"

"Have you ever seen the glass insulators on phone poles?"

"Yeah?"

"There used to be an old, empty farm in the field out behind our house when I was a kid. There was a downed phone pole out by the old farmhouse frame. We used to hunt for the insulators in the ground by that phone pole and take them to the antique shop."

"Oh yeah?"

"Yep. The green ones and the blue ones were worth the most money, at least they used to be."

"How much?"

"We'd get two to three bucks for the green ones, and five bucks for the blue ones. If we found a really nice blue one, he'd give us seven bucks. That's not bad for a kid."

"Especially way back then."

"Hey," Dad protested, "are you calling me old?"

Mom grinned. "Yeah, but you're a cute old man. Anyway, what happens if he actually *finds* real treasure. I've heard the same treasure rumors, about money from some bank robbery being stashed somewhere on our property.

Dad gave her another long kiss. Gross! "Then I guess we hope he's a good money manager. We told him he could keep it. I always tell *him* he's got to keep *his* word. How would I look if I went back on *my* word?"

"A man of your word, that's why I love you so much." She leaned in for another kiss. That was all I could stand. I left them to their disgusting display and went on down to the basement. Mom had some old garden tools down there that I thought might help us dig for more coins.

CHAPTER FORTY-FOUR

The Three Rules
(Told by Mary Fran)

Monday after school, I rode into town with my mom while the boys waited at Big Oak. Mom was making her biweekly trip to the Agway store to get chicken feed, and I told her I wanted to see if an old coin I'd found was worth anything. She dropped me off at the antique store while she went to pick up the chicken feed. To say I was unprepared for what Mr. Cosgrove at the antique shop would tell me, might be the biggest understatement since General Washington said he was a little leery of Benedict Arnold.

I'd promised myself that I wasn't going to get all excited and act like a dumb kid if the coins were worth anything. It's funny how kids never want to act like kids. So anyway, I was braced to stay calm, but with every word out of Mr. Cosgrove's mouth, the good ship Stay Calm drifted further and further out to sea.

"Where did you come across this coin, little lady?"

"I saw it by the side of the road while I was riding my bike," I said, with what I hoped was an honest look.

"What road was that?" he asked casually.

This guy thought he was some sort of master of

interrogation, but he was no match for my parents. I knew immediately that he was probing for information.

I lied. "Fedora Road, just outside of town."

"What's your name again, Honey?"

"Mary Fran."

"Mary Fran what?"

It made me uncomfortable that he wanted to know all of this, but I figured we'd have to deal with him eventually, when we cashed the coins in, so I thought I ought to tell him the truth. "Mary Fran Barker."

"Well, Mary Fran Barker, this coin isn't a dollar, it's a twenty dollar coin. To be specific, it's an 1864 twenty dollar, gold double eagle."

Twenty dollars!

My knees turned into wet noodles. I didn't know exactly what 1864 twenty dollar, gold double eagles were, but I knew we had nine of them and I was pretty darn good at math.

"Does that mean that thing is worth twenty dollars?"

Mr. Cosgrove smirked and chuckled. Then he paused for a moment. I'd seen adults smirk like that before, it was the 'you poor dumb kid' look.

He's trying to figure out how little he can get away with giving me for this coin. I thought. *Maybe it's worth thirty or forty.*

He pulled out a book, looked something up, and put the coin on a scale. Then he took out a pocket calculator and pecked at a few keys. He looked at me and smiled.

"Young lady, 1864 double eagles contain 0.9613 ounces of gold, making them among the largest, heaviest gold coins ever to circulate in the United States."

It must be closer to forty.

I didn't know what that meant, but I sure liked the sound of it. "Yeah? Is that good?"

He glanced at the numbers on his calculator again. "At current gold prices, this coin is worth about three hundred eighty-four dollars by weight. But all old US Gold Coins are worth a premium over their actual gold value," he said as he handed the coin back to me. My knees were so wobbly now, that I was holding the counter to stand up.

"What's a premium?"

He smiled. "That's just a fancy way to say it's worth more than its weight in gold. It has extra value just for being old."

"So it's worth *more* than three hundred eighty-four dollars?"

"Sure is, little missy. You've made yourself a nice little find. You wouldn't be interested in selling it would you?" I was mute. A girl can't multiply three hundred eighty-four by nine, and speak coherently at the same time. "Mary Fran? Mary Fran? Hey, are you okay?"

"Oh … yeah. Sorry mister. I was a little shocked."

"I don't blame you. So … uh, would you be interested in selling it?"

"I better think about it some before I decide."

"Fair enough, but promise me you'll come back here first if you want to sell it. I'll give you a fair price."

"Sure thing, Mr. Cosgrove," I said as I slipped the coin back into my pocket, reflexively patted the outside of my pocket, and headed toward the door. "Thank you very much, sir."

For some reason, when I left the store, I thought Mr. Cosgrove was following me and I looked back over my shoulder. I was apparently being more than a bit paranoid. He was leaning back in his chair and on the phone, just like he'd been when I came in.

When I got back to Big Oak, the three boys were sitting in the shade, staring at the place where the old milk can had been. I was kind of surprised. We had all agreed that nobody would do any digging unless everyone was there, but I sort of expected the boys to be digging without me.

I was met with several seconds of slack-jawed silence when I told them what Mr. Cosgrove said.

"That's more than thirty-four hundred dollars," Josh said.

I was impressed with his quick math skills, but not half as much as Miss Hoyler, his math teacher, would be. I didn't think he was that smart.

"Holy smokes!" Mickey added.

"How much is that each?" Eli immediately asked. He was a man after my own heart.

"It's more than eight hundred fifty dollars each, Eli, eight hundred sixty-four, to be exact."

Josh was up and pacing now. "And that's only for the nine coins we've found."

"Do you really think there's more down there?" Mickey asked.

I smiled at him as I stood up. "Well Mickey, there's only one way to find out."

We weren't exactly equipped like the world's best archaeologists, but we had some tools there. Somehow, with no more than a few pieces of twine, Eli had managed to get a shovel and a screen that he used to gather bait, from his house to Big Oak on his bike. Mickey brought a shovel, and I brought a steel rake from home. Josh had a garden trowel, a garden claw, a wet cloth for cleaning the coins, and a Ziplock bag. I remembered hearing somewhere that trying to clean the coins wasn't good for their value, but I'd tell Josh about that later.

After further excavating 'The Milk Can Site' for an hour and a half, we had thirty-one more coins, an agreement to meet here tomorrow after school, and four dazed looks. We replaced the soil from the hole, tamped it down, put a big rock over the spot, and reconfirmed the three rules of our partnership before going home for the day.

We split everything we find into four equal parts.

Nobody digs unless all of us dig.

And we don't speak a word of this to anyone else, not even parents. The mouths stay shut.

CHAPTER FORTY-FIVE

The Kid on the Milk Carton
(Told by Josh)

Tuesday night was nothing like Sunday. My homework Tuesday was to know the words on my vocabulary sheet, and for math, to do all the even-numbered problems at the end of chapter fourteen. I had done the math homework in school, at lunch, and felt like I already knew eighteen of the twenty words on the vocabulary sheet. I'd looked up the definitions of the two words in question, 'abduct' and 'malevolent', before I got on the bus home. I worked on memorizing the meanings of those two words on the short ride home, while I changed into my play clothes, and while I rode out to Big Oak with my excavation tools.

Eli and I arrived at *about* the same time, but just for the record, I got there first. Mickey got there third, which meant that Mary Fran was going to get there last. Paydirt! Boy, were we going to give *her* the business! For the first fifteen or twenty minutes, I was busy thinking up all of the ways I could let Mary Fran have it for being the last one to get there. It never occurred to me that something might not be right. I'm pretty sure Eli and Mickey were doing the same thing.

It was Mickey who first voiced subtle concern. "I wonder

what's keeping her."

"Probably the same thing that kept me on Sunday," I said. "I bet her mom gave her a hundred extra chores when she got home."

"This isn't like her." Eli said. "Do you think we should go over and help her get them done?"

I gave him the side-eye. "Well that's funny pal, none of you came over to help *me* like that on Sunday."

I understood that Eli probably wanted to help Mary Fran because he was sweet on her, and I actually *hoped* he was starting to grow on her. But there was no way I was going to miss the chance to bust his chops. Even at eleven, we understood the parameters of the guy code, and this was an egregious violation.

Eli hung his head in a proper display of contrition, and we went back to silently worrying about Mary Fran.

Ten minutes later, Eli was pacing, Mickey was picking at his fingernails, and we'd all moved from mild concern to actual alarm.

"What time is it?" I asked.

"How are we supposed to know?" Eli said. "Mary Fran's the one who always has a watch on."

I glared at him, but he was right.

"It's probably nothing, I bet she just went somewhere with her mom," Mickey said, "should we just start digging now? We're splitting everything four ways anyhow."

"We don't dig unless *all* of us are here," I said, "that's the rule! Here's what we're gonna do. Mickey, you and Eli ride over to Mary Fran's house and see if she's there. I'm going to ride over to Grout Brook and then back to *my* house. She's lost track of time before, gabbing with Aggie or my mom. You know how girls are."

"Yeah, that's probably where she is." Eli said, trying to sound calm, but the concerned look in his eyes told me his truth.

What I saw in Eli's eyes, made me worry more too. This was the first time it occurred to me that something *really* bad might have happened to Mary Fran. Maybe someone knew about the coins we'd found and decided they wanted them. Maybe Mary Fran blabbed and somebody grabbed her. She'd shown the coin to Mr. Cosgrove at the antique shop the day before. Maybe he decided he wanted it. But all he knew was that she had one coin that was worth less than four hundred dollars. Would he grab a kid for four hundred dollars? That was crazy! I tried to push these dark thoughts from my mind. I tried to sound unconcerned.

"Yeah Eli, I'm sure it's nothing. Now let's go find her. Everyone meet back here after we check our assigned places. She'll probably be here waiting to make fun of us, thinking she was first to get here."

"Okay," Eli said, and he and Mickey jumped on their bikes and took off down the trail towards Nichols Corners Road.

"I'm sure it's nothing," I kept saying to myself in a soft whisper as I walked toward my bike, "I'm sure it's nothing."

I picked up my garden claw and got on my bike, still whispering, "I'm sure it's nothing," as I pedaled up the trail toward Grout Brook.

Although I didn't see anyone at Grout Brook, as I got off my bike the short hairs on my arms, and the back of my neck, stood up. This had never happened before. This place had always been a refuge, not a place of unease.

"Mary Fran, Mary Fran … Mary Fran," I called into the woods.

There was no answer, just the echoes of my shouts.

I got back on my bike and pumped the pedals as hard as I could, up the trail towards our house. I found Mom out back, taking down laundry.

"Hey Mom, has Mary Fran been by here?"

I noticed Mom looking down at the gardening claw in my hand, but she didn't mention it.

"No, Honey. Don't you kids always meet down at Big Oak after school?"

My heart was thumping like a bad flat tire, but I downplayed it.

"Yeah, it's just that she's a little late getting there. We thought maybe she stopped here and got hung up gabbing with you. She's done that before you know."

Mom smiled. "Guilty as charged, but not this time. She's probably there by now, honey … wondering where you are."

"Yeah, you're right Mom. I guess I ought to get going."

CHAPTER FORTY-SIX

Blue Danger
(Told by Mary Fran)

Where was I when the boys were looking all over for me? It's a long story. That Tuesday was a big day. Like any other afternoon in November, the boys and I planned to meet at Big Oak as soon as we got home from school. Why was today special? We'd found forty valuable coins up until then, and we were going to be digging for more today. This was the day we could go to bed rich.

Mickey got to my house very quickly. He'd brought his play clothes to school and changed into them before he got on the bus. When he got home, all he had to do was toss his school clothes on his bed, grab his bike, and go. He stopped to see if I was ready, but I wasn't. He offered to wait while I got changed, but I told him I'd only be five minutes behind him and he should go ahead. I wasn't worried about being left out. The boys weren't going to do anything without me. Nobody digs unless all of us dig.

I went back inside, finished getting changed, got on my bike, and started for Big Oak. At the end of my driveway, I looked to my right, then turned left. When I looked to my right, I'd noticed a dark blue car sitting on the side of the road. I thought

178

that was odd. He was just sitting there, halfway between our driveway and Mickey's. I'd never seen anyone sitting there, on the side of our road with their motor running before, but I didn't give it a second thought. There was treasure to unearth. I looked back to my left and saw Eli turn into the woods up ahead of me. I knew Mickey was ahead of Eli, and Josh was probably there already. We'd be digging up more treasure in less than ten minutes.

I stood on the pedals and started cranking them hard up Nichols Corners Road. I was hopelessly behind Mickey, but my ego wouldn't allow me to accept that I couldn't catch him.

Halfway to the trail, I caught sight of the big, dark blue car creeping up beside me in the corner of my vision. The car didn't pass me or fall behind. It just kept pace. We were on opposite sides of the road, and there was another car coming towards us from the other direction, so I didn't turn my head to look at the blue car right away.

The hairs on my arms stood up.

After the other car passed between us, I turned to look over at the blue car and was surprised to see Hannah's father, Mr. Brady, Chief Brady as he'd corrected me before. For an instant, I was relieved that it was someone I knew, but only for an instant. The look on his face changed all of that. His eyes were wild with what looked like rage. But why? I'd never done anything to him. The only time we'd ever met was when I visited his sick daughter. Then I thought that maybe it wasn't rage, maybe it was fear.

Is Hannah sick again?

We were fifty feet from the DeLeon Road intersection now. I hadn't been able to turn off onto the trail because he'd kept the car even with my bike. He pointed to the side of the road. He wanted me to stop. He *was* the Police Chief, and I sort of knew him. The only reason I was uncomfortable was that look on his face. I convinced myself that he was just worried over Hannah. Yes, Hannah had probably taken ill again.

I pulled over onto the dirt on the side of the road and got off of my bike.

He stopped a few feet behind me, but across the road. He got out of his car, flashed a quick smile, and started talking to me, coming closer all the while.

"Hi Mary Fran, do you remember me? It's Mary Fran, right? Hannah just can't stop talking about you."

Hannah wouldn't have gone on about me that way. We were friendly, but we weren't that close. I immediately threw away my explanation that this was about Hannah. My stomach churned. The look on his face, and the fact that he left his car running with the door open made me uneasy. Why was he stopping me? I hadn't done anything wrong, and if I *had* done anything wrong, he would have come to my house. And he kept coming closer to me. Mom had always taught me never to let a stranger get within arm's length. I rolled my bike half a foot, so it was directly between us. He was the Chief of Police, and he wasn't exactly a stranger, but he sure was *acting* strange.

My heart battered at the inside of my chest. I backed away, dragging the bike sideways with me. "I remember you, sir. Did I do something wrong?"

"No, Mary Fran," he *kept* coming, "I just recognized you and wanted to say hello."

That was when he lunged at me. When I tried to take a step back, I stepped on my shoelace, staggered back, lost my balance, and began to fall. He grabbed my arm. Still smiling, he pulled me to my feet.

His smile, along with the fact that he'd just saved me from falling should have put me at ease. But I also remembered how Aggie reacted when I told her I'd been in his house.

In an instant, Brady's eyes caught fire and his grip on my arm tightened. Aggie's reaction flickered through my mind, and his next words told me I needed to get loose ... *now*!

"Where are the coins, Mary Fran?" My mouth hung agape in stunned silence. His grip on my arm tightened even more. He asked again, this time with a snarl. "Where are the *coins*?"

My eyes were locked on him, but just then, I heard a clicking sound, paws on blacktop. There was a snarling sound, Brady's eyes got really big.

"Aaaiiieeeee,!" he yowled, and let go of me.

I followed his eyes down to his left, lower leg. It was *Penny,* her teeth deep in his calf, snarling and shaking her head. Brady shook his leg and tried to punch her twice, but Penny ducked his punches. Still shaking Brady's leg, her eyes shot to me for an instant. Her eyes seemed to be telling me to run. I jumped on my bike and obliged.

As I pedaled hard up the road, a car turned off of DeLeon Road and towards me. That car passed. I looked back over my right shoulder. Penny was gone, and Brady was running back to his car. When I turned right on De Leon Road, towards Josh's house, I veered across to the left side of the road. Brady would catch up in seconds and I wanted to have a lane between us.

The Corey's driveway was about half a football field away when he pulled even with me. He looked over at me with that same wild look. I gasped when he started to veer his car across the road towards me. He was trying to run me off the road, and I had nowhere to go.

But just as suddenly, he turned his head to look up the road, and jerked his car back onto his side of the road. When *I* looked ahead, I saw why. Two cars were coming from the other direction. The lead car was close, but the other was far enough down the road that it gave me a second to think. The second car would pass us before I could reach the Corey's driveway and I'd be trapped again. I acted fast and took the only option I saw. I pulled my bike into a skidding 180-degree turn in the roadside dirt, and pumped hard back toward Nichols Corners Road, where we'd just come from. It was a maneuver Eli had taught me. The cars coming towards Brady kept him from making an immediate U-turn and following me. He had to wait, and I had time to turn onto Nichols Corners Road, but I knew he'd be back on my tail in no time.

I was going to turn into the woods, which were on my *left* now, so I stayed on the right side of the road to make my turn wider, and easier. I was in the same lane as Brady now. He had turned onto Nichols Corners Road, and was coming up fast behind me. He was closer every time I looked back over my shoulder. There was no more looking back. The turn into the woods was feet away. The engine roared louder and closer.

CHAPTER FORTY-SEVEN

A Serious Possibility
(Told by Josh)

I was physically ill with worry. I felt like I'd drank a glass of grapefruit juice after drinking a glass of milk, (don't try this), and I was *not* sure the end result wasn't going to be the same. There were now two fewer places remaining for us to find Mary Fran safe and sound.

I muttered Mom's words to myself. "She's probably there by now."

I was torn. I wanted to pedal as fast as I could. If Mary Fran was in trouble, we needed to get to her, but I was in no hurry to find her somewhere ... beyond help.

That was when Mom rejoined the debate from her place in the back of my mind, whispering silently.

She's probably there by now.

It hadn't been long ago that I was pedaling down this same trail, hoping against hope that I wouldn't find Mary Fran standing there, waiting for me at the end of my ride. Now, I'd give anything to find her standing there.

The harder I pedaled, the faster I cut through the air. It was my own personal wind, there to dry my tears as they slid down my

The Hanley Chronicles

It was possible that she'd gone to Grout Brook after I checked it the first time, so I swung past there once more. She wasn't there, so I took the cut-across trail over to Big Oak. At first, I was alarmed when I got there and Mickey and Eli weren't there. I wondered if this malevolent thing had claimed *them* too. I paused my thoughts for a moment when I realized I'd just used one of the vocabulary words I'd been studying. Then I went back to worrying about my friends.

Wait! Eli and Mickey probably didn't stop at the road. Maybe they kept going and pedaled down Nichols Corners Road to her house. I bet that's why I got here first. Maybe they're all down there, laughing and talking to each other.

I jumped back on the pedals and started down toward the road. I didn't have to go far. I wasn't a hundred feet down the trail when I heard the clattering of approaching bikes. My heart dropped when I only saw two people pedaling up the trail towards me. It was just Mickey *and* Eli.

"Any luck, Josh?"

"No," I told Mickey, "I checked my house, and Grout Brook twice. How about you guys?"

"Nope."

"I was worried 'cause I got back to Big Oak before you two." I explained, "You two must have gone all the way out to her house, huh?"

"Nah, just to the road. Halfway there, Eli's bike threw its chain. We had a little trouble getting it back on."

Little did we know that minutes ago, while the three of us were riding toward each other on the path, Mary Fran had made her skidding U-turn on DeLeon Road and was just now turning back onto Nichols Corners Road.

"Do you think we ought to go check her house? She *could* be there."

"I guess it's possible," Mickey said, "but I doubt it. She was about to get changed when I first stopped at her house. She said she'd only be five minutes behind me. But it can't hurt to check. It *is* where she lives."

Mickey and Eli turned around and we started down to the

183

road. We'd gone a hundred feet down the path when we heard it, the revving engine, the squealing tires, the shriek, the thud, and a pause. Then we heard the revving engine again and the squeal of tires, their skin being torn off by the road. Next came the silence, the blaring silence. I knew immediately that it was Mary Fran's shriek. I'd heard that shriek while we played at least a half-dozen times by now. And that terrible thud! It reverberated through me like the grand finale of the Fourth of July fireworks. We all stopped and stared at each other with slack jaws for a few moments. Then we jumped back on our bikes and tore down the trail as fast as our legs could take us, praying that we'd find Mary Fran unhurt down at the road.

When we emerged from the trail, I could smell the burnt rubber from the squealing tires. The first thing I *saw* was the crumpled red bike lying across the double yellow line in the middle of the road. Then I saw the tire marks on the pavement. They seemed to go on forever.

As I rode down that path in the woods, I had been lying to myself, promising myself that I was going to see something good, something reassuring. But everything I saw twisted my stomach into tighter knots and caused my heart to claw its way further up into my throat.

I got off my bike, dropped it at the edge of the trees, ran down to the road, and reluctantly started walking toward Mary Fran's bike. I should have been running, but I was afraid of what I'd see. Mickey and Eli followed me. Every step felt like it was taken with cement legs. I wanted to be approaching anything in the world other than what was in front of me.

As we came up over the slight rise in the road, my heart sank. I saw the small crumpled figure of a person lying near the roadside ditch. My stomach was churning, and bound into a Gordian knot at the same time. I wanted to turn and run. But this was Mary Fran! She was one of us. Of course, the waters of Grout Brook came immediately to mind. Would a bottle full or a couple of cups be enough? We didn't have any bottle or cup anyway. What if she was already dead? Could the waters of Grout Brook do anything for a dead person? I replayed that sickening thud in my mind. Dead was a serious possibility. There was no more time for debate. She was going in the brook, and she was going there now!

I walked faster. The lump in my throat grew as I got closer, not just because I was getting closer, but because seconds were passing, and I wasn't seeing any movement.

CHAPTER FORTY-EIGHT

Sweetheart
(Told by Josh)

Finally, when I was no more than thirty feet away, I could see what I desperately did *not* want to see. All doubt was removed. That puddle of humanity on the side of the road *was* Mary Fran.

"Come on you guys," I blurted out as I ran over to her.

The good news was she was moving. Well, she had finally moved. She was clearly not okay, in fact, she was a train wreck. Her hair was bloody, her right eye was swollen, her chin had a gash an inch and a half long, her face was dirty, and she had a big welt across her right cheek. There was more than a trickle of blood coming from her mouth and a pool of blood under her head. I chose not to look at the back of her head. I didn't want to see where all that blood was coming from.

"Oh my God!" Eli cried out.

"We have to get help!" Mickey yelled.

I leaned in close, so my mouth was right next to Mary Fran's ear. "Mary Fran, you are *gonna* be okay."

"It hurts," she said in a half-moan, half-whisper, followed by some other things I couldn't understand.

I was vaguely aware of a car pulling to a stop on the road

186

behind me. A car door opened and closed, I heard footsteps approaching, and then a woman's voice.

"Oh my God, what happened?"

"What do you *think*?" Eli screamed. "Somebody hit her with a car!"

"Okay, okay, you boys stay here with her. Okay?" the woman backed toward her car. "I'm going to go for help. Okay? Okay?"

"Yes! Yes!" I shouted, "Go!"

Later, I felt terrible about yelling at that lady that way, but I was scared, I just wanted her to go so we could help Mary Fran.

I knew what we had to do, but I also knew there was no way any adult would let us do it. Normally, you never move an accident victim. I'd learned that in Boy Scouts in my old neighborhood. This, however, wasn't a situation that you'd call normal. Amy's dog, Miss Shea's dog, Mrs. Devitt, Hannah Brady, and at least a half-dozen other people had all been brought back from somewhere near death's door. Grout Brook had proven itself. I was as sure as I could be that I was doing the right thing.

But this was Mary Fran, and she wasn't a little bit sick. She was wrecked! I'd be lying if I told you the tiny, nagging voice of doubt wasn't whispering in my ear, telling me that we could be paralyzing Mary Fran forever … or *worse*.

As soon as the woman's car disappeared over that rise in the road, Mickey, Eli, and I sprang into action. I grabbed under her arms as best I could. Her shirt was soaked with blood and she was hard to hold on to.

"Okay," I barked out, "Mickey, you get one leg and Eli, you get the other. Eli, Eli! Come on Eli! Quit bawling and let's *go!*"

Eli snapped out of it and grabbed Mary Fran's right leg. As we picked her up, she let out a sound that cut through me like a January wind. I can only describe it as a half-yip and half-wheeze, then she went silent. I wondered if she had just died, but there was no time to check.

The road was paved and easy to walk on, even while we were carrying Mary Fran, so we covered ground relatively fast. Since Mickey and Eli were shuffling backward and I was going forward, I was able to see down the road, where the woman had gone for help. I saw her turn into Eli's driveway.

"Eli, is anybody home at your house?"

Blood was still dripping from somewhere on the back of Mary Fran's head.

"No. My dad's at work, and my mom's at Miss Edy's house."

"Good," I said as we reached the trail in the woods.

The good news was that no one was home at Eli's. It would take the woman a little while to realize that, and go to the next house. The bad news was, the next house was Mary Fran's. Mrs. Barker *was* home, and she'd know Mary Fran had just left home, and figure out that it was probably Mary Fran who was hurt.

"Turn here," I said, "we're taking her to Grout Brook."

I'm sure they knew where we were going, but they were walking backward, and I didn't know if they could see that we'd reached the trail.

As soon as we were off the road, things got more difficult. The path was only two or three feet wide and Eli and Mickey, backing up side by side, couldn't both be completely on the trail at the same time. Also, we were all moving at different speeds. A root grabbed Mickey's foot, and he started to stumble backward. Fortunately, Eli knew instinctively, to stop, which we both did. When Mickey fell, Mary Fran did not, only her leg did.

She wheezed. "It hurts."

I was relieved that she was still alive. I looked behind us. We weren't far enough up the trail. We could still be seen from the road.

Come on, Mickey! I screamed in my mind. *Get up! Get up now, Mickey!*

But my actual words were gentle. "You okay, Mickey?"

"Yeah," he said, struggling back to his feet, "I think so."

Come on Mickey!

I kept looking back and forth between the road and Mickey. He finally had Mary Fran's leg again.

"Okay," he said, "let's go."

We were moving again, but slower now, painfully so. We didn't want anybody to fall again.

With my back to the road, all I could do was listen for a car. If I'd been facing the road, I probably wouldn't have been able to see much anyway. My eyes were filled with tears and I couldn't see.

"Eli, do you see anyone down on the road?"

"No, but I can barely see the road now."

I exhaled. If Eli couldn't see the road, then people on the road couldn't see us. Just as I started to feel like maybe everything had a chance to be okay, Eli's heel hit a root and *he* went down in a heap. But Eli didn't jump back up as fast as Mickey had. Eli's elbow had hit a rock.

Oh God, Eli, not you too!

He grabbed his elbow and rolled around on the ground with a grimace. Then I heard a car coming up the road from the direction of Eli's house.

Get up, Eli! I wanted to scream, but I bit my tongue. He was obviously hurt.

Blood still dripped from the back of Mary Fran's head. I looked behind us. There was no one coming up the trail, but that didn't mean that there *wouldn't* be. They'd *seen* us come out of the woods there. Where else would they think we had gone?

Eli got back to his feet, but he was still holding his elbow.

"I can carry both her feet," Mickey told Eli, "you just be my eyes."

There was no way Mickey could do that. We'd barely been managing with the three of us. But I admired Mickey for volunteering to try.

"No! I'm okay, Mickey. Let's get going."

Thank you, Eli ... Thank you.

We were moving again, and I could hear the gurgling of Grout Brook. Mary Fran's breathing was raspy now, and I was getting worried. Her eyes were starting to flicker. I'd seen this several times on TV, and it was never good. Were we running out of time?

"Hang on, Mary Fran," I whispered, "hang on!"

The next two minutes seemed like an eternity, but the gurgling of Grout Brook was getting louder. I could smell the water now, and the trail was getting wider. We were almost there.

As the ground started sloping toward the water, Eli and Mickey started going faster. They were going to fall and I had to run to keep from dropping Mary Fran on the rocky shore. The split-second decision I made to veer right saved Mary Fran and I from landing on top of Mickey and Eli. We splashed into the water.

When I surfaced and stood up, the other two guys were holding Mary Fran by her upper arms, but she was face down. Now I could see the terrible gash on the back of her head that I'd been trying not to see.

"Turn her around," I yelled, "she has to be face up to breathe."

They had her turned over by the time I sloshed through waist-high water to help hold her head up. When I got to her, there was a dense flow of red water meandering downstream from the back of her head. I brushed her hair out of her face and gently shook her as I talked to her.

"Come on, Mary Fran, wake up." I caressed her cheek. "Come on sweetheart, open your eyes."

Mary Fran did as I asked, and while I was tremendously relieved to see those big brown eyes open, I immediately wished it hadn't been right after I called her sweetheart.

I got that from my mom. She used that word all the time when she was worried about someone, even the dog. After all of this passed, there would be no explaining that to Mary Fran. But for now, I was just glad to see her weak smile, and hear her feeble two-word answer.

"Hi Josh."

CHAPTER FORTY-NINE

Unscathed
(Told by Josh)

I helped Mary Fran to her feet. "Are you okay?"

"Why are we in Grout Brook … in our clothes?"

"*Are you okay?*"

"Yes, yes, I'm *fine*. Now can we please get out of the water?"

Eli, Mickey and I watched like three lions eyeballing an antelope, but we didn't view Mary Fran as lunch. We all just watched to be sure she really *was* okay.

"What are you goofs looking at?"

I wasn't going to answer her. I didn't really *have* an answer.

"We just want to be sure you're okay," Eli said.

She was a little wobbly as she walked out of Grout Brook, but she got up onto dry ground on her own. She wouldn't allow any of us to help her. Yep, she was being appropriately difficult. Aside from that wobble, Mary Fran seemed back to her old self.

"Okay? How come you keep asking me that? What happened?"

The gash on her chin was gone, and so was the swelling of

her eye. The water had washed the blood from her hair, and the welt on her cheek was gone.

"Come over here, let me see your head."

"Not until you tell me what happened."

"Nope! No deal. You let me check your head first."

She stomped her foot and offered her usual commentary on me. "You're impossible!" But she did as I asked. I carefully searched through the wet hair on the back of her head, and found no trace of the huge cut that had been oozing blood minutes ago. I turned her around, put my hands on her shoulders, and gave her a Cheshire grin.

"You seem to be perfectly fine except for one small problem."

"What? What? What's wrong?"

"Your mouth works. You can still talk."

"Mickey and Eli burst out in laughter. Mary Fran harrumphed.

"Very funny! Now can you *please* tell me what happened?"

"Come on and we'll show you," I said as I stepped in front to lead the way down the path.

"Okay, Sweetheart," she said. "Lead the way."

Sweetheart? I gulped.

My head jerked around like a trout who'd just had a hook set in his mouth, and judging by the smirk on her face, maybe the trout would have had a better deal than me. Mickey and Eli laughed.

Yeah, Mary Fran was okay.

We heard the sirens as we walked through the woods, and down toward the road. We could see the emergency lights through the trees when we got close enough. Ten feet from the opening we heard voices.

"I'm telling you, she was right here and she was badly hurt. There were three boys here with her."

"Mrs. Edmond," the deputy said, "don't take this personally, but ... have you been drinking?"

The woman sounded insulted. "No, I most certainly have *not*! Look at the blood! Look at the bike! I'm telling you, I left her right here with three boys to go call you!"

When we stepped closer to the opening in the trees, Mary Fran's jaw fell. There laid her crumpled bike, now on the side of the road, not far from the Sheriff's car and a red Ford Bronco.

The color drained from her face. "I got hit by a car?"

"And you were hurt really bad," Mickey said.

I felt compelled to add my commentary. "I was worried you might die."

"My *bike*!"

"Don't worry about the bike, Mary Fran. *You* were wrecked!" I said, "until we got you into Grout Brook."

"Can we fix my bike?"

I shook my head in disbelief. All she could think of was her dumb bike. *Yeah,* I thought, *she's alright.*

"From what I saw when we were down there getting you, no way. But forget about that. You're lucky to be alive."

"Hey," the woman who was talking to the deputy looked up and pointed at us, "there they are. That's them right there."

The second woman, the deputy, and the two EMTs all looked at us. I recognized the second woman right away. It was Mrs. Barker.

"Mary Fran!" she screamed and ran to her daughter to hug her.

"Hey, you kids." The deputy gestured for us to come down to him. "Come down here for a minute please?"

I wanted to turn around and run, but we walked down toward where they were talking.

When no one was home at Eli's, the woman in the red Bronco had *indeed* gone to Mary Fran's house to call for help. Mrs. Barker had immediately feared it was Mary Fran who'd been hurt, and rode up the road with the woman in the Bronco. When she saw Mary Fran in her torn jeans and bloodstained shirt, she lost it.

"Oh my God!" she said, "Mary Fran, are you okay?"

Mrs. Barker was apparently trying to hug Mary Fran's innards out. "Yeah Mom, I'm okay."

She didn't appear to hear her daughter's answer. She patted Mary Fran's head, ran fingers through her still wet hair, and checked every piece of exposed skin for damage.

"That can't be. Look at that pool of blood!" insisted the Bronco woman. She acted like she was losing points in some dead kid scavenger hunt.

"Did somebody hit an animal?" I asked with a dumb look on my face, trying to offer an explanation for the blood on the ground. "Maybe Mary Fran fell in the blood."

Mary Fran's mom was now crying, and still running her hands up and down Mary Fran's body. Poor Mary Fran was mortified when her mother lifted her shirt to check for damage.

"Mom, stop! The boys are *right* here."

That was when the female EMT stepped forward. "Let me check her, ma'am. I can do it inside of the rig. You can come in with her and she can keep her privacy. Okay?"

Mrs. Barker looked down at Mary Fran to see if she was okay with that. Mary Fran, now red-faced, nodded.

While they were climbing into the ambulance, the deputy turned to us. "Any of you boys see what happened?"

We all shook our heads no.

I put my hand on Mickey's shoulder and spoke up. "We were in the woods, sixty or seventy feet back on that trail. We heard the tires skid, a thump, and that was all. Then we tore out down here to see what happened." Mickey nodded for emphasis, or support, or something.

"How'd all of you get wet?" the Sheriff asked.

I figured I'd better speak up before Eli opened his fool mouth and ruined a good story. "We'd all been swimming in the creek before everything happened. Mary Fran left the creek first, said she was heading home."

The deputy appeared to be a little suspicious of my explanation. He might not have been buying my story.

"She probably got going down the trail too fast and bailed from her bike so she wouldn't get killed, and the car probably took out her bike," I added. "You know how nutty girls can be."

That made him smile, and his smile made me exhale. I looked over at Mary Fran's bike to see if maybe we could fix it, but it was *definitely* a goner.

Just then, Mary Fran, her mom, and the EMT came out of the ambulance and the EMT shook her head in disbelief.

194

"She seems to be in perfect health. I can't find a mark *on* her. But maybe you should let us take her to the hospital anyway … just to be sure."

"I don't understand why. If you say she's okay … I mean, we can't afford an ambulance bill. We're just getting by."

"Well there could be damage that we can't see, and Mary Fran can't feel yet."

At this point, the deputy interceded. "And Mrs. Barker, nothing involved with this will cost you a nickel. In our state, all injuries resulting from any motor vehicle incident will be covered by *someone's* auto policy, even if it was Mary Fran's fault. And you can believe me, we *will* find whoever hit your daughter … or her bike. It sure wasn't her fault that they took off!"

"Oh," was all Mary Fran's mom could muster.

The EMT added one more thing. "If you want, you can sign a waiver to decline the ambulance service, and drive Mary Fran to the hospital yourself. After the deputy gets Mary Fran's statement, you really *should* get her checked at the hospital. They can run some tests that we can't. It would help me rest easier."

CHAPTER FIFTY

Eyewitness
(Told by Josh)

We stayed there until Mary Fran's mom left to get their car and take her to the hospital. I guess we stayed just to be extra sure she was okay. We watched as she told the deputy what she remembered about the whole thing, which wasn't very much. This wasn't unusual at all. Every time someone had been close to death before the waters of Grout Brook brought them back, they seemed to lose most of the last hour of their memory. The same thing happened to Mrs. Devitt, and the others.

"I remember being scared. It seemed like something was chasing me. I guess my bike got smashed somehow."

He didn't need Mary Fran's memory to know that, her bike gave him that information the moment he pulled onto the scene.

"What else?" he asked.

"Blue ... I remember blue."

"A blue car?"

"I don't know. The color blue is just in my mind."

The deputy allowed a flicker of frustration to show on his face, but Mary Fran didn't see it. It didn't matter anyway. The bike would once again provide the answer. The vehicle that demolished her bike had left navy blue paint as a souvenir.

"Is there anything you *do* remember about the incident that I should know?"

Now it was Mary Fran whose face showed frustration. She wanted to be helpful. She wanted to remember more, but there was just nothing there. She shook her head.

"So no one here saw what happened?" We all gave him shrugs and blank looks and shook our heads no.

"I saw what happened," came a female voice from the tree line behind us, "I saw it all, and I know who did it."

The deputy looked up and past us at the same time we all spun around. As I'd suspected from the voice, it was Aggie. She came down from the path and up the road to where we were standing.

"Okay, who are you?"

"Agnes, I'm Agnes Granger. People call me Aggie."

He jotted her name down in his notebook. "Well, Aggie, what did you see?"

She pointed at the trail where she had just come out of the woods. "I was done swimming, in the stream up that trail there, I'd walked down to my car."

The deputy looked around. "What car?" he asked, probably wondering if it was going to be blue.

"It's right down the road," she pointed in the direction of Eli's house. "It isn't blue. It's white, go check and see if you want."

He walked down the road to where her car was parked amongst the trees in the thirty-foot long pull-off.

He wrote down her plate number, and came back up the road to us.

"Okay, so go ahead. What did you see?"

She nodded toward Mary Fran. "I saw this little girl. She had just stopped her bike over there on the left shoulder," she pointed across the road, and then to the crumpled red bike that was now on the side of the road, "that bike there."

"Okay."

"The man in the blue car was across the road from her. They looked like they were talking."

"Car? What kind of car?"

"It was a big, navy blue car. Maybe a Buick or a Crown Vic. I couldn't hear what they were saying. They were too far away. When he got out and walked across the road I recognized him right away. It was Chief Brady."

"Eric Brady? Chief of Police, Eric Brady?"

"Yes, sir. That's who it was!"

"Are you *sure*?"

"I'm as sure as the day is long! Who else around here is that tall? And I'll tell you another thing. Rance Lowery didn't kill Caleb Hanley. Rance Lowery didn't kill anybody."

"Wait, what are you saying?"

"I'm saying that Chief Brady killed Rance Lowery *and* Caleb Hanley. I saw the whole thing."

The deputy shook his head, as if to clear cobwebs. "Okay, let's just take care of *this* accident for now. Let's get back to what you saw today."

His voice had the same tone as my mom's voice did whenever she didn't believe me. My heart sank. Aggie hadn't wanted to get involved because she would end up having to give her age. She took that chance and told the authorities what she'd seen, and it looked like it was going to be worthless. He didn't seem to believe her.

"I *saw* Chief Brady grab that girl. Then a black dog came out of the woods, around the car and bit him. That was when the little girl pulled free and took off. She had a head start because he had to run back to his cruiser." The deputy was taking notes furiously. "By the time he got it going, she was turning right on to DeLeon Road, then she disappeared behind the trees. He sped off after her, and I thought I had seen all I was going to see."

"You saw more?"

"Yes! She must have managed to pull off a U-turn somehow, because it wasn't a minute later that she turned back onto Nichols Corners Road and was pedaling like mad toward me. Brady wasn't far behind her. He turned back onto Nichols Corners Road, came right up behind her, and bumped her. The bike wobbled and flipped and that poor girl bounced across the road like a rag doll." She glanced at me and I saw the flicker of a smile before she ended her account of what happened. "It's a miracle she's alive."

My jaw must have hit the floor. I could not believe what I was hearing. She was saying that Eric Brady, the Chief of Police in our little town, was a double murderer and a would-be child abductor. Was this true? The very man who was supposed to keep us safe? The worst kind of criminal? If we couldn't trust the people who were there to keep us safe, could we ever feel safe again? A chill slithered down my spine. I looked up at the deputy taking notes, and wondered about *him*.

Eventually, everyone was done giving their statements, and I'd settled myself down. Mary Fran's mom pulled up in her car, picked Mary Fran up and took her off to the hospital. Mrs. Edmond left in her red Bronco. The deputy put Mary Fran's bike in his trunk, turned his car around, and waved as he drove off.

As we boys walked back down the road to the path in the woods, Aggie was almost back to the parking cutout where her car was. When we turned off the road to go up onto the path, she looked back at us. We waved to her. She waved back and disappeared behind the trees. As we picked up our bikes and walked into the woods I took a deep, cleansing breath, and shook my head in disbelief.

"I can't believe Mary Fran's alright," I said, remembering the way she looked when we first walked up to her lying in that road. That was when I noticed that I was still shaking.

CHAPTER FIFTY-ONE

Freak Woman
(Told by Josh)

Mary Fran had been to the hospital and come back with a clean bill of health, and the incident on the road was the topic of conversation for the next two days. We talked about the reports on the local news, and since Mary Fran had little or no recollection of what happened, we tried to help her piece things together.

Despite the fact that Mary Fran's loss of memory made her all but useless as a witness, Brady was arrested Tuesday night, and it was all over Wednesday's newspaper and T.V. news. Aggie's statement led Sheriff's deputies to Brady before he could get rid of any evidence of the collision. The scratches and red paint on his car were all they needed to see. He was eventually charged with, and convicted of, attempted kidnapping, felony hit and run, attempted robbery, and conspiracy to commit robbery.

Late Friday afternoon, Mary Fran, Eli, and Mickey left Big Oak to get cleaned up. They were coming over to my house for dinner. I decided to go over to Grout Brook for a bit, while I waited for them to come back through. When I got to the brook, Aggie was there.

"Hey, Miss Aggie."

"Hey there, Josh! How are you doing?"

"I'm doin' great. I'm so happy Mary Fran is okay."

Aggie looked sad, which confused me. Why would Mary Fran's safe return make Aggie sad?

A tear slid down her cheek. "I wish I could have gotten *Caleb* down to the water in time."

Now I understood. I felt bad. How could I have forgotten that she'd gone through the horror of Mr. Hanley's murder? He was someone she loved! I never knew she actually *saw* it happen.

I was hesitant to ask the next question, but only for a moment. There isn't enough reluctance in a dentist's waiting room to tamp down the curiosity I felt. "Did you *really* see Mr. Hanley get killed?"

She gazed into the water and slowly moved her feet back and forth. "Yeah," she said in a raspy whisper, "I saw it happen."

"*Geez!* I would have been scared half to death."

She wiped another tear from her cheek. "I was, Josh. Believe me, I was."

"Well, how did it happen? What did you –" I caught myself. This was hard for her and I was thoughtless to push her. "I'm sorry, Miss Aggie. Never mind."

"No, no. That's okay, Josh." She wiped away another tear. "I should have spoken up a long time ago. I'll tell you the story." More tears. "On that day, I was at Caleb's house. But I didn't have my car. He'd taken me to dinner the night before and we were out so late, I just stayed the night. There was no tomfoolery you understand. I slept on his sofa." I nodded, not fully understanding why she told me that, or what she meant by tomfoolery, and she continued. "Caleb's work was farming, so the only place he had to be in the morning was here, doing his chores. He was going to take me home after he did his morning work on the farm. I was doing some housework for him. He wasn't a messy man, but he was a man living alone. No matter how neat a man is, there are some things a man just doesn't clean right.

"I was dusting in his living room and I'd pulled the curtains closed because the sun was getting warm. I was doing the top of the curtains when Brady came, and like anyone would be, I was curious to see what a police car was doing here. I peeked out between the curtains and saw Brady get out of his cruiser with a shotgun. That made me nervous, but when he leveled that gun at Caleb I got *really* scared. I thought he was arresting Caleb. Caleb started shouting and gesturing with his hands. I couldn't hear him, but it was pretty clear that he wasn't happy."

My eleven-year-old eyes widened. "Wow! What happened next?"

"Well, all of the sudden, he just shot Caleb. That shotgun blast was the only part of the whole thing that I actually heard. It was so loud.

I grabbed my shoes and ran out the kitchen door. I thought Brady might come in the house for some reason, and I didn't want to be here if he did. You know how the house is on higher ground than the field out back? Like on a little rise?"

"Yeah?"

"I ran out back behind that rise, crawled on my hands and knees as fast as I could, over to the tree line."

"Oh man!"

"When I got to where I could watch from the trees, I saw Mr. Lowery's truck coming down the driveway. Brady was coming out of the barn and he dropped a pickax next to Caleb. That was when he saw Mr. Lowery. When Mr. Lowery parked his truck, he waved and walked toward Brady. Brady shot him too. Poor Mr. Lowery never had a chance. Brady put the pickax back in the barn, went to Mr. Lowery's truck, got the shotgun from the gun rack in the back window, and dropped it on the ground next to Lowery."

"Why'd he do that?"

"He wanted everyone to think Mr. Lowery killed Caleb."

"Well, it worked," I said. "When we looked at the old newspapers in the library, they all said Lowery *did* kill Mr. Hanley."

When I looked back up at Miss Aggie, she was crying again. She wiped away the tears, patted me on the shoulder, and smiled. "Don't worry, Josh. I'll be okay."

"Are you going to tell them everything you saw?"

"I really want to. It seems like the right thing to do, but that deputy I told the other day didn't seem to believe me. Besides, I don't want everyone to know how old I am. If I go to court, I'll probably have to show somebody my ID, and I don't want the whole world on my doorstep to see the freak woman who's over 140 years old."

CHAPTER FIFTY-TWO

In Retrospect
(Told by Josh)

As it turned out, Aggie *did* go to the authorities and tell her story, which wasn't very good for Chief Brady. At first, I felt kind of bad for him. He said the only reason he killed Hanley and Lowery, and went after Mary Fran was to get money for an experimental treatment for Hannah. Insurance companies don't pay for those.

But like almost all criminals, he wasn't as clever as he thought he was. Kind of like kids, trying to lie to their parents. Once Aggie talked to the police, they looked at their evidence again. It didn't take very much investigation for the State Police to figure out that something was very wrong with his account of what happened. You see, Brady said he drove up on the scene and found Mr. Lowery not far from Mr. Hanley, who was dead on the ground. One look at the crime scene photos showed that Mr. Lowery's tire tracks were made on top of Brady's tire tracks. That meant Brady was there first. That little detail convinced the State Police Investigators to look a little closer. When they looked at Mr. Lowery's shotgun, there was no gunshot residue on the gun at all, none in the barrel or the breach. Lowery's shotgun had never been fired, ever! His wife backed this up with a sales receipt. The gun was her birthday present to her husband, which she'd given to him two days earlier. He told her that he was going over to show it to Caleb and see if he wanted to go with him to try it out when the weekend came. So it became clear that Rance Lowery had not killed Caleb Hanley ... never even got the chance to shoot his new gun. Lastly, there was the imprint of the pickaxe in the dirt next to Mr. Hanley, but there was no pickaxe, and Brady's fingerprints were on the pickaxe in the barn. If the pickaxe had been next to him, why would Brady move it? When all of this came to light, a lot of us wondered how they'd missed it all. But as I got older, I came to understand. It was a small town. He was the Chief of Police. They didn't really investigate, they took dictation for him.

Brady agreed to plead guilty to the two murders in exchange for a life sentence in protective custody. That's solitary confinement for people who the other prisoners want to hurt. I guess that would be moderately better than a needle in the arm.

The investigators who nailed Brady had acquired his phone records in the course of the murder investigation. Those phone records happened to connect him to Mr. Cosgrove from the antique shop. It turns out that he had called Brady right after Mary Fran left his shop.

Cosgrove eventually pleaded guilty to conspiracy to commit robbery, and agreed to cooperate with investigators in exchange for a reduced sentence. His information helped them put Brady in prison, and that helped Cosgrove get sentenced to five years probation instead of fifteen in prison. But he also lost the town's trust and had to sell the antique shop.

Considering the fact that *one* of us kids had already been attacked over the gold coins, the judge closed the courtroom to help ensure our safety. Part of Mr. Cosgrove's plea agreement was that he keep his mouth shut. If the Judge found out that he said *anything* about us and our coins, his original fifteen-year prison sentence would be enforced.

When Aggie went in and reported what she knew, she didn't end up having the problems she anticipated. Remember Hillary Shea, the town clerk who had the sick corgi, and who is close friends with Amy? At Amy's request, she was able to 'cut through some red tape' and get Aggie a new copy of her birth certificate. However, it seems she made a helpful mistake about Aggie's year of birth. I guess one good turn deserves another.

By then, our tally was ninety-two gold double eagles, which by Cosgrove's numbers were worth a little more than $35,000.00, plus a 'small premium'. Mr. Cosgrove's lack of honesty, however, was not limited to conspiring to have little girls jumped and robbed. What he neglected to tell Mary Fran at the antique shop, was that this *small premium* he spoke of, was about $430.00 more per coin.

At current auction prices, our particular gold double eagles were actually worth an average of $814 apiece. So our treasure trove, which by winter, consisted of one hundred forty-eight coins, was worth more than $120,000.00. Cut into four equal parts, this amounted to $30,118.00 each. To this day, Mary Fran thinks there are fifty-two more double eagles down there somewhere. She did more research and says that shipments in those days were made in bags of two hundred coins.

To everyone's credit, we all did a great job of keeping our mouths shut. Considering that Mary Fran almost lost her life in the Brady Incident, maybe our silence wasn't all that remarkable.

Of course, our silence no longer included our parents. When Mom and Dad found out the actual value of what we'd found, they installed themselves as my financial advisers. I mean, they kept true to Dad's word. My share of the money *was* all mine, they were just going to help me decide how to use it to my maximum benefit. I guess I can't complain, I got a new bike and a new baseball glove out of the deal ... oh, and a college education. The majority of Mickey's and Mary Fran's shares went to their college educations too.

I think Eli's parents recognized something in Eli that the rest of us also knew. Eli was a prince. He was a great guy, a hard worker, and we all knew he was going places ... but we also knew none of those places would be college. Eli's money was saved for him and when added to the other money he'd earned, working through his high school years, he had enough money to make a down payment on an old auto repair shop in town. He ended up knowing more about cars than *anyone* I've ever met. Eli's Auto

Repair is now the biggest auto repair business in three adjoining counties. He now has five locations. That treasure put Eli on the road to doing what he loves to do for the rest of his life, which will be a very, very long time.

Hannah Brady was adopted by the Burns family, a wonderful family in our town with more kids than a goat farm. Against all odds, and with a boatload of love, they gave Hannah a great childhood. She ended up going off to college and returning to become our county coroner.

I'd like to hang around and tell you more stories all day, but I have a lot to do. I have to take Max and Penny for a walk. Also, Mom and Dad called, and are nagging me to bring the kids over for a visit. I also have an editor who's going to flip her wig if I don't finish the changes she sent me, and Amy just called to remind me that Eli and Mary Fran will be over with those unruly kids of theirs in an hour and a half.

Yeah, that's right, Eli and Mary Fran, and me and Amy. At first, Amy was a little weirded out by the idea of dating a man she had known as an eleven-year-old kid, but I persisted, and I *was* the only person in town who knew her actual age. Actually, it was easy. I just made sure she had a good supply of Grout Brook water, and after a while, I caught up to her. It wasn't hard. After all, what woman *wouldn't* drink some special water that could keep her young forever?

I've got to get going now, but maybe I'll tell you more later.

<<<< End >>>>

www.ingramcontent.com/pod-product-compliance
Lightning Source LLC
Chambersburg PA
CBHW020630180626
46816CB00003B/889